DANGER IN THE SUN

DANGER IN THE SUN

Helen McCabe

CHIVERS

British Library Cataloguing in Publication Data available

This Large Print edition published by AudioGO Ltd, Bath, 2013.
Published by arrangement with the Author

U.K. Hardcover   ISBN   97814713 4705 4
U.K. Softcover   ISBN   978 1 4713 4706 1

Printed and bound in Great Britain by
TJ International Ltd

CHAPTER ONE

Lauren came to, rubbed her neck and blinked. However comfortable the deep leather seats of Gary's Land Cruiser were, she'd managed to lie awkwardly and crick her neck. She moved, grimaced with the pain, then opened her eyes full into a deep-pink dawn. The landscape was bathed in a rosy light making the French countryside look like a high definition movie. They were speeding between rocks and gorges. On one of the highest peaks, Lauren could see a castle clinging to the very pinnacle, forged into the rock face.

'Nice view,' she said, then she reached down for her bag. Gary turned from the wheel and smiled as Lauren started rummaging in its depths. She looked up conscious of his admiring eyes. 'How long have I been asleep?'

'Three hours. You slipped against me, so I propped you up.'

She winced and was about to retort he hadn't made a very good job of it, then decided it would be better to keep her boss in a good mood. He was notoriously bad-tempered in the morning, especially if they had an early assignment.

'I'm sorry,' he added.

'What for?'

'We should have stayed the night

1

somewhere, off the auto route, but you know what I'm like.'

'Yes! So what changed your mind?' she asked.

He shrugged. 'I like getting to places quickly. Time is money.'

Lauren looked out of the window again. He had plenty of money. In this case, he was sure to have another agenda. If he'd really wanted to stop, he would have. She also sensed whatever he was hurrying to the sun for was something she wasn't supposed to know about.

When he'd suggested the stopover, then taken the phone call, which he'd answered in a series of quick fire responses, she'd been relieved, because the break in their journey would have made things difficult. She'd have had to say 'No' to him outright.

Maybe he'd got the message she wasn't keen—or thought he'd win in the end—but, in reality, she knew his decision was nothing to do with her. She retrieved her compact mirror and winced at her reflection.

'You never look a mess,' he said, grinning. 'I wish every girl looked like you in the morning.' He took his hand off the wheel and reached over. She looked down at the tanned, strong fingers closing over her hand. He must have felt her withdrawal, because after a slight pressure, he returned to his driving.

Lauren put on her sunglasses, which did a great job masking her expression. She leaned back and the sunlight streamed in, washing away her tiredness with its dazzling warmth.

The rocks had been replaced by gently-sloping hills and tiny fields full of vines. Red tiled roofs made the houses look like the Spanish ones they had photographed recently for another of Gary's travel books. She knew how lucky she was to be the personal assistant of a global entrepreneur, but also that her value was measured in how well she managed the publicity for the book side of his business. He had a surprising talent for writing travel books which tied in exceptionally well with his extensive dealings around the planet. Much of Gary's other business was a mystery to her—and she knew that's how he wanted it. Being part of it was exciting, but she was aware now of its drawbacks, certainly more so than when she'd first joined Grey & M Associates.

Lauren glanced at him. He'd said in her job interview that he'd expect her to drive him around sometimes, but that hadn't happened yet. He had several cars, but the powerful seven-seater Land Cruiser was the work horse. It was big to handle, but she'd been fairly annoyed when she hadn't been offered the wheel although he'd been happy to let Paul drive about three hours ago. However, his photographer's driving was less frenetic and Gary had lost patience. Now, Paul was cat-napping, slumped across the back seats, his camera right next to him. It was an extension of him and, like every professional photographer, he was ever ready to capture that one special shot. He had a wariness about him that told Lauren he hadn't always been so laid back, but he certainly knew how to handle a camera.

She sighed. Sometimes, she wondered what the hell she was doing travelling the globe with two men who purported not to have a past. Gary's details could be looked up in Wikipedia and *Who's Who* and he was listed as, *influential in both the business and travel sphere. Author of a number of successful books in both areas . . .*

On the other hand, Paul was a regular guy who appeared to live for the moment. He was useful to have around and he knew how to party. How the two of them met she didn't know, or how they got on, seeing as they were so different. She was sure though that they had mutual secrets, although Gary had let one slip; that Paul had an ex-wife.

Lauren knew Gary had two previous marriages—but no children. Lauren had neither, except some regrets born of a couple of past relationships that had never come to anything. At present, she had no time for one. However, when she'd accepted the challenge in Gary's eyes, after he said, 'I promise you the trip to the Riviera is not going to be all business, Lauren,' the smile that followed might have won another girl's heart, but not hers. As far as she was concerned, she intended their relationship remain on a professional footing. At least, she'd have Paul to back her up. Lauren knew he wasn't keen on his boss getting together with her either.

Lauren liked Paul. He could be relied on to break an awkward silence with a joke and make things better than they generally were, especially when everyone was on edge. When matters became serious, Paul was indispensable. How many times had she been glad he was coming along on this particular trip, the reason being she didn't want to be alone with Gary. Her boss was good company, paid her a lot of money and the perks were seriously good when they didn't become too personal, but he was also driven, unpredictably moody and secretive.

She remembered how happy she'd been when her interview had been successful. What had attracted her when she had seen the advertisement was the opportunity to travel. *Businessman seeks experienced personal assistant. Excellent salary and prospects. Must be prepared to travel at short notice.*

Could it be a year ago since she had taken the job, she thought? She'd won it in the face of heavy competition, but she had both publishing and marketing experience as well as a business degree. She also had a good grasp of three languages. French was her best. She was practically bi-lingual, given her background. She knew she'd been lucky, but she'd also discovered that Gary had a high turnover of PAs. She'd learned a lot since she'd started working for him, but she'd had no chance of knowing everything as his business was so complex.

At present, things were difficult and once or twice she'd considered giving in her notice, but then she'd decided she was tough enough to cope. She felt she was up to the challenge. What she was doing looked great on her CV and when she'd had enough and learned enough, she'd most likely move on. When days were really bad, she always told herself things would get better. Lauren sighed at the thought of what was to come. She'd never been to the French Riviera, although she loved France and visited her grandma's old home there several times, but she knew she probably would never even have the chance to look around in the style she enjoyed now unless she had been working for Gary.

It would be so easy to go along with what she suspected he wanted from her at present, but Lauren had her principles. She worked for him and that didn't mean she was going to end up sleeping with him. It would have made things very difficult and would be extremely unprofessional. She had an unshakeable instinct it would be the wrong thing to do and also the suspicion that was what had happened to several of her predecessors. Besides, Gary wasn't the kind of guy she went for. She was still waiting for the right man to come along and she was sure that man wasn't her boss.

Maybe she'd meet her ideal man on this assignment which he'd told her was just another commissioned travel book. They were heading for Port Grimaud where Gary had taken a villa. She remembered him coming off the phone, grinning.

'Hey, Lauren,' he said, 'a couple of months on the Riviera will do us both good. Grim's more private than St Tropez, which is full of celebs and wannabe starlets. I hate the place. But you'll love Grim! Remember this could be a holiday for both of us.'

Lauren wouldn't forget that emphasis on *us—both of us.* At that moment, she'd wondered if that was the time to say she was handing in her notice, but she was confident she could handle the situation. She could manage him and if the fun became too serious then she might well call it all off, but two months in the Riviera was a very tempting prospect.

Her present dilemma was trying to decide whether Gary really felt anything for her or that her attraction lay in the fact she hadn't fallen into his arms like every woman he charmed. Plenty of girls wanted a relationship with a man who figured on the broadsheets' rich list! Lauren knew she couldn't go on stalling for ever and, finally, she might have to make a clean break. Gary didn't like losing, but she was optimistic.

That's my problem, she thought to herself as they drove on into the sun.

'Hey, Paul. Man up. We're stopping.' Gary barked.

At that precise moment, he swung the heavy vehicle into the slip road. Lauren heard the stage-managed groan from the back. In front, the traffic was beginning to queue and Gary swore under his breath.

She leaned back and studied her reflection in the small mirror. Tousled waves of hair framing an oval face. Skin lightly golden coming from the last expedition to Spain. *Phew,* she thought. *Let's hope this one's not as manic.* Gary had been late on his deadline owing to other commitments as he called them, and she'd spent too many hours checking and re-checking the whole document before it was e-mailed to his editor.

Lauren applied a touch of bronze lipstick and ran her fingers through her mane. She looked behind. Paul was hastily combing through his thick, shaggy, brown hair with one hand and trying to fasten his shirt buttons with the other. It was only at that moment she noticed the scar deep under his hairline. It looked like it had been a serious head injury. She looked away, but she knew he'd seen the question in her eyes.

Gary pressed the ignition button and the engine died. He leaned back still looking cool, his blond hair flopping over his forehead. *See Gary, think Hugh Grant,* was what Lauren had first thought. Now she knew he hadn't the film star's fluid foppishness. Gary was hard-edged. You only had to be at one of his Board meetings to know that.

'I don't want a full meal,' he pronounced. 'Café?' They nodded. If she and Paul had wanted the restaurant, it would have been just the same. Gary liked his own way about everything, but then, he was paying!

'Fine by me, Boss. How about you, Lauren?' asked Paul, who was looking behind him at the time. She nodded. Gary opened his door and stretched his long lean frame. Opening hers, she was hit by the cool, dawn air. As she put out her leg, Gary was round, waiting for her to jump down from the high chassis. She avoided his arms, then shivered as the wind caught her.

With Lauren between them, the trio walked across the tarmac towards the low complex of buildings flying the flags of the European Union. Then Lauren caught the unmistakably French scent of hot croissants, strong coffee, wine and garlic. At the same moment, the wind cut into them.

'Mistral,' said Gary. 'Blows all night, whines through the trees, disappears into the heat of the day. Straight from Africa.'

'Bit like us then, Boss,' joked Paul.

He and Gary had spent the last two weeks in West Africa, while she was tussling with the

9

Spanish edits. That trip had nothing to do with this present Riviera book, but was referred to as 'just a reccie for some other business'. There had been no photographs, which wasn't what usually happened, but she'd been told nothing, which annoyed her as she'd presumed he'd be working on a West African assignment which he'd dump on her at the last minute. And he evidently hadn't wanted her along either. Just Paul.

'Mistral!' Lauren mused. 'I like that word. It's so—French.'

'You mean romantic,' Gary said.

'Maybe,' she quipped.

Paul squeezed her elbow. Lauren knew the photographer understood the situation between her and Gary. He saw it as a game and had even made a bet with her that Gary would win! Lauren was confident she wouldn't lose her money, because everything was in hand.

As they reached the café, Paul was looking behind him again.

'What's the matter?' she asked.

'The usual,' he replied. 'Wash and shave.'

'Not in the car park,' she quipped. She knew Paul better than that. He was the least smart man she knew. That's why she'd been surprised the first time she met him. He looked scruffy, except for his ring, which he wore on the middle finger of his left hand and never took off. The stone was brilliant, but the claw setting was ugly and ostentatious. She asked about it once.

'That's an unusual ring,' she'd said. 'Where did you buy it?'

'I inherited it,' he said.

'Is that a diamond?'

'Russian,' he'd said. 'Made in the lab.' She didn't understand until she looked it up. Evidently, Russian diamonds were rare and much sought after, mined in inhospitable places like Siberia, but synthetic ones were manufactured in the lab. Ever since then when it had caught her eye, she was pretty sure it was cubic zirconia. Lauren loved jewellery.

'Come on, you two,' Gary called over. They joined him and were all about to cross well ahead of a massive slowing lorry, when a red Ferrari shot past them with a screech of tyres and swung into a parking space opposite.

'Idiot!' shouted Gary, as he caught Lauren's arm to steady her. She could feel herself shaking. Then the right hand door opened. A tall, tanned man wound himself out and hurried over.

'Pardon, monsieur, je regrette . . .'

'What was your driver doing? Trying to do kill us?'

The Frenchman was about to reply when the driver of the Ferrari stretched up and out. Lauren had forgotten it was a left wheel drive. The woman was model-beautiful with a sheet of blonde hair, a white belted raincoat, matching silk designer scarf and slim legs encased in expensive leather boots.

'Great pins,' murmured Paul in Lauren's ear.

Gary was staring at her in silence. As though oblivious of their notice, the girl walked straight past them. Then the Frenchman shrugged and looked at Lauren. Up until then, she had not encountered such an enchanting smile. The stranger's casual clothes and the cut of his jacket had a style that said St Laurent.

She didn't find only his clothes interesting. Looking at his profile, he reminded her of the statue that Paul had photographed in Athens, the one that Gary had used for the frontispiece of his Greek travel guide. Instead of hard stone curls, this man had glossy black hair cut in the French way so that it seemed hardly cut, golden skin, dark eyes. Everything about him reminded her of all the rich young men she had met while she had travelled the world with Gary. There was one difference however, and it was only a quick impression—he was sad.

'Pardon, mam'selle.' His dark eyes studied her directly with a challenging stare, which at the same time was full of fun. She looked away, feeling naïve and foolish and, a second later, Gary grabbed her arm hard. Lauren pulled away from him. Immediately, the Frenchman turned and followed his haughty, travelling companion.

'I thought they'd given up that mam'selle

stuff,' Gary snarled to no-one in particular, swore then exploded. 'Women drivers!'

'Good start to the day,' Lauren murmured to Paul, but he wasn't listening. He was taking a photograph of the Ferrari.

'One hundred and twenty thousand dollars. What a beaut!'

'Give me a Lamborghini any day,' snarled Gary.

CHAPTER TWO

The café wasn't Gary's style, but Lauren liked it. Travelling and travellers had always fascinated her. The smell inside the café was irresistible, the aroma of fine French cooking issuing from the restaurant which adjoined it.

'It's busy,' she said, looking round. Gary took no notice.

'You sit there.' He indicated a small table positioned behind a cheese plant. Ordering people about came naturally to him. 'Coffee and a selection of croissants?'

He strode off and she watched him go with a sigh of relief. It was good to be out of the Land Cruiser, although it was comfortable. She felt almost too tired to eat, but she was sure Paul would help her out. He was nowhere to be seen. The stand-up tables which were a fashion in France were already surrounded by travellers, drinking red wine even at that early hour. At the ordinary tables, the occupants were dipping their rolls into their coffee bowls, then sucking them. She relaxed. It was good being away from Gary even for a moment. With him, you always needed to be on your guard.

She watched him fidgeting in the long queue, looking round impatiently and sensed his thoughts. He and Paul would have to stand—and he was regretting now that he hadn't gone to the restaurant. She knew he wouldn't admit to making a mistake. By now, she'd realised that he wasn't a particularly nice person and it was no wonder that he'd been divorced by two wives!

The profuse cheese plant which had grown to tree-like proportions waved above her, but seated behind it was an excellent spot to people-watch. On the snowy cloth before her was the menu and Lauren picked it up and smiled.

Compared with motorway restaurants at home, the choice of food was dazzling. As she skimmed through the *hors d'oeuvre*, all of a sudden she was very conscious of someone watching her. She glanced sideways and saw four men eating. All were wearing shades and looked like clones in identical black roll-neck sweaters and jeans. One gave her an imperceptible nod and she glanced away quickly. They looked like thugs. She was glad she wasn't on her own, because she had a very strong feeling the man's nod was not only Gallic familiarity, but probably something more sinister.

Lauren looked past them into the restaurant where candles were lit and a white-aproned waiter was bustling between the tables. There they were—the couple from the Ferrari! Of course, the café wouldn't be their style. The girl had taken off her raincoat, revealing a superb low-cut white dress which showed off the deep lustre of her tan. She was laughing in a brittle fashion, but what she was saying seemed not to be making an impression on her handsome companion. His jacket was off and his shirt was equally designer. He wasn't smiling.

I knew he was sad, thought Lauren, as he continued to listen to his garrulous companion. Lauren kept watching what was going on between them under her lashes, wondering where they had been and where they were headed. She didn't want to glance sideways as the four men were still there, probably leering at her behind their sinister shades. All at once she wished Paul would hurry back from wherever he'd gone. Then a moment later, Gary was handing her a large plate.

'Thank you,' she said, looking at the mound of croissants and wondering how she was going to get through all those. She would have given anything to be seated in the restaurant in the model girl's place, listening to the handsome stranger.

*   *   *

'Jean-Luc, you're not listening,' said a peeved Simone Belleville. He leaned over and took her hand, knowing that she'd be satisfied, because she loved confessing to him or boring him silly with her particular brand of Parisian retail therapy.

'I was—in the beginning,' he said, 'but you know, Simone, I have no real interest in shopping.'

She withdrew her hand. They sat in silence, until she began to tell him about a recent fashion show she'd attended. He sighed, but she didn't notice. Simone thought she was witty, delightful, even *charmante,* but she was no longer any of those things to Jean-Luc. She failed to delight him now because she had betrayed him in the past. He had forgiven her, but he told himself he was still with her not out of weakness but for reasons of his own, which were both selfish and necessary.

So far he had found no-one else whom he admired or wanted particularly. Simone was hell, but she had the ability to keep some interest in ordinary life going, so the two of them dined out and sipped their wine and she continued to flirt with him because it was some time since they had slept together and she was

16

sure she would get him back into her bed.

He had known Simone since they were teenagers and his late father had struck up a business relationship with her father, Maurice Belleville. He and Simone had history, which was, at present, foremost in his mind. He would continue to listen to Simone's chatter—for a while—but he could see it coming to an end in the near future, when he had found out more about the business he had been handed when his father died.

His son had been a disappointment to him as he had not shown a particular interest in the diamond trade. Jean-Luc was wealthy enough to do anything he wanted, but he owed it to his father to settle his affairs in a proper manner. At present, that was Jean-Luc's overriding concern. To keep Simone on side and do nothing that would hinder his uneasy relationship with Maurice until he discovered the truth about the Belleville business dealings.

However, as Simone babbled on, his eyes continued to flick towards the pretty, white cast-iron table with its even prettier occupant, who was now guarded by the surly Englishman and the photographer. He had been watching her for some time. The girl thought she couldn't be seen behind the greenery and kept glancing at him. Did she think he wouldn't notice her after their brief encounter outside? He admitted he was interested in who she was and what business she had with the two men, who were accompanying her. Also where she was headed, but he had too many pressing matters on his mind right now.

He concluded as he finished his coffee that if he was to meet the unknown girl again it would be Fate. Jean-Luc smiled. He did not believe in destiny so it was particularly unlikely that would happen, but in any case it was the most pleasant diversion he'd enjoyed in some time. She was gorgeous, stirring within him an excitement he'd almost forgotten.

*　　*　　*

Lauren finished her breakfast, but her mind was not on anything except the Frenchman's surreptitious glances. She knew it was ridiculous but she'd like to see him again. Gary and Paul were standing behind her, engrossed in conversation and the four men were still seated at the table. At least she was confident that she was rid of their unwanted attention.

She scrunched her serviette and looked up as the French girl flounced past her, followed by her companion. She caught his dark, flashing glance once more—and then he was gone, disappearing through the swing doors.

'Come on, darling,' said Gary, looking at his watch. 'You haven't eaten much. Time to go!'

Lauren bristled, then frowned at him. She had ticked him off before for calling her 'darling' and he'd stopped, until that morning. He was grinning too, which made her more annoyed.

She finished her lukewarm drink and gathered her things.

Paul was staring. 'Are you going to leave all those?' He indicated the the croissants. He'd had two already. She nodded, so he picked up the ones she'd left.

'Don't forget the butter,' remarked Gary sarcastically.

'Thanks, boss,' replied Paul and stuffed both butter and jam packets into his jacket pocket.

'Don't get run over by a Ferrari this time,' said Gary.

'What a way to go,' joked Paul as they walked out into the fresh morning air. All at once, they heard the roar of the powerful engine and Lauren saw the red Ferrari nose its way out through the traffic lanes and shoot away.

*　　　*　　　*

The rest of their journey was easy. They swung off the auto route before it wheeled away to Nice and Cannes. The sky was now as blue as a picture postcard and the sea—Lauren always marvelled at the turquoise of the Mediterranean—lapped on unspoiled white beaches close to the road. Palm trees fringed the strand and beautiful villas crouched against the hillsides, almost obscured by sweet pines and flowery bushes.

'Which one's ours?' asked Paul, looking up at the villas.

'Are you kidding?' replied Gary. If anyone but Gary had said that, they'd think they weren't headed somewhere good, but Lauren knew better. He liked his comfort and their accommodation would be up to expectations.

'Hey, over there. Look. Tropez!'

The Land Cruiser was skirting the Bay of St Tropez, its red roofs and mock towers stark against the foamy, white froth on the Mediterranean.

'So that's St Tropez,' she said looking into the distance. She smiled inwardly as she remember the last time she'd phoned home and told them where she was going on her latest assignment. Her father's reaction was, 'Remember me to Bardot if you see her!'

'Look at all those tourists,' groaned Gary. Multi-coloured umbrellas were now dotting every space on the beaches.

'Serves you right, boss, for coming at this time of the year,' grinned Paul.

'I'd like to go there,' said Lauren.

Gary looked surprised. 'I thought you hated crowds.'

'I do, but there's something about the look of it.'

'You mean boutiques! Are you asking me for a raise?'

'I might be!' She heard Paul snort.

They swung on to Port Grimaud, another playground of the rich and the wealthy, but less crowded. The approach to the town was again typically Southern French: a railway bridge festooned with advertising slogans and strings of fairy lights swinging in the breeze. The village was all pink walls, red roofs, crazy alleyways and forests of tall masts.

'Did they throw in a yacht with the villa?' quipped Paul.

'Not quite,' replied Gary.

Paul shrugged at Lauren. A moment later, they were in the central part of the village. 'Little Venice' was how the tour operators billed Grimaud. Practically all the roads were inlets from the Med and the wide basin was a haven for yachts of all kinds. Gary stopped in the square and produced a residents' permit, which he stuck on the vehicle.

'It really is like Venice,' said Lauren, looking around

'That's why I like it,' replied Gary.

Lauren grimaced. When she was in Venice with Gary, she'd been very new to the job then and she'd found his attention flattering, which had been dangerous. She supposed she'd been flattered that the boss thought so much of her and had chosen her out of so many hopefuls and she'd almost—almost—gone to bed with him. They'd kissed and taken candlelight dinners beside the Grand Canal and had done a lot of the things lovers do in Venice.

As she looked round, she was thinking what had stopped her. Probably Paul with his wry humorous way of coming between them at exactly the right time. Gary hadn't been happy, but he hadn't sacked him. It seemed that Paul could say anything to him and he still kept him on. She couldn't work it out at present and assumed Gary needed him.

Their villa was just across the little bridge that spanned a wide canal off the square. Inside, it was perfect.

'Wonderful light here,' said Paul, staring around, then out of the windows.

Gary showed her the room where she'd be sleeping. 'Like it?' His bad mood had changed to charming.

'It's great,' she said, 'but I'm so tired.'

They'd come down fast, hours of driving without a break until the stop on the auto route. Gary was in a hurry and Lauren didn't know why.

She could see the white yachts tossing at their anchors, but she found she just wanted to lie down and sleep. After he left, she showered and was ready to crash out for a couple of hours.

There a knock on the door. She answered, still in her robe.

'You look lovely,' Gary said. She knew what the look meant. She was in for a battle. 'Can I come in?'

'I'm just going to lie down.'

'That's what I mean. Wouldn't you like company?' he said.

'Please don't,' answered Lauren.

'I don't understand you, Lauren. We've been together a long time—we like each other . . .'

'Sometimes,' she replied. His face changed. 'It's just that I don't care about you in that way.'

'Do you really have to love someone to go to bed with them, Lauren?' She could hear the irritation in his voice, it was always the same. Fending him off was getting her down.

'Maybe I do. I just don't . . .' It wasn't true, but she wouldn't let him know.

'Sleep around? You're in the minority.' His voice was bitter and he was looking a lot less pleasant than a few seconds ago.

'Gary, I'd rather we keep things on a business footing.'

'I can see that,' he said, backing off. 'It's your choice. I feel the same about you as the day I hired you. Like I did in Venice.'

'I'm sorry, Gary. Now, if you don't mind, I'd like to go to sleep.' She was closing the door.

'So that's it?'

'Yes,' she replied, thinking that he'd probably sack her now.

'Well, I'm not going to stop trying,' he said. 'I'm not going to see you shack up with someone who—'

'Hey, Boss,' she heard Paul's voice with relief, 'You need to come and look at this.' A moment later, Paul was beside him. 'Everything ok?' He looked from one to the other.

'Of course,' said Lauren, 'I was just going to take a nap.'

'Sensible,' said Paul. Lauren could see Gary was seething. 'Boss?' Gary turned, his face set and charged off. Paul winked at Lauren.

'Thanks,' she mouthed.

As she went inside and threw herself on the bed, she wondered what the hell she was doing here and what she was going to do, knowing that it was her own fault she was in this position. Sometimes, the man was insufferable, like a child who couldn't get what he wanted. And he isn't going to get it. *Just how long can I hold out?* Lauren asked herself. She felt really frustrated and if things didn't get better in a couple of weeks, she would hand in her notice, however much she loved the job.

Later, lying under her smooth Egyptian cotton sheets, she thought of the Frenchman on the auto route and wondered what he was doing at that very moment.

*   *   *

The Bay of St Tropez glittered. In the yacht harbour crammed with masts and pennants the boats lay, tossing at their anchors, the darlings of their millionaire owners.

The girl with the sheet of white-blonde stretched out in a lounger on the deck of a particularly pretty one, which was dwarfed by the monster beside it, the property of a Russian billionaire.

L'Hirondelle, Jean-Luc's's yacht, had a presence its crass neighbour lacked, its polished wooden deck proclaiming a vintage which the other could only aspire to.

She put out a manicured foot, examined the varnish on the nails and yawned. She was wearing the tiniest of bikinis which she had bought herself in her favourite boutique in Tropez and she would have preferred to have been enjoying some retail therapy rather than a boring business meeting at her father's villa, but he would be tetchy if she didn't turn up and she was feeling too lazy even to cajole him for the new dress she had seen in the same shop.

Jean-Luc was boring this afternoon, too. He had work to do as well. That's what he said anyway. She glanced towards the upper deck where she could see him talking to François. His yacht master was talking volubly and showing him something. He looked nervous. Simone Belleville smiled because she knew her new conquest was indeed nervous. He'd keep his mouth shut, but she didn't have to worry because if Jean-Luc found out he'd been spending time with her instead of doing his job, he knew he'd be out.

She looked up again. They were both very good-looking in different ways, but François had no money. The Mistral was annoying her hair and she felt a tiny bit cold. She couldn't be bothered to go and slip into something less revealing, so she put up a lazy arm and a crew man came running.

'Fetch me my cashmere wrap,' she said. 'Over there. On the bench.' He looked pathetically happy to be useful.

The engine was purring beneath them. They had an hour or so before she and Jean-Luc went their separate ways that evening. She waved to him and he came down, not leaping to her command like the sailor, but in that easy, laid back manner that annoyed her. He regarded her with the same expression as when they'd played together at his aunt's country house when they were children. A *what do you want now, Simone?* look.

'Do we have to go?' she cajoled, patting the lounger beside her. 'It's too hot to work.'

'You know you do. You're getting lazier, Simone. Why are you in a bikini, if you need a cashmere wrap? It doesn't make sense. If you're cold, go and get dressed—and stop treating my crew like your butler. Yes, we do have to go. Your father needs you and I need to get on with some work. I'll take you out when we go to Monaco. Yes? You can lose some money on the tables.'

'You should calm down, Jean-Luc. Enjoy yourself more. You don't need to work, you said that yourself. Have you bought my birthday present yet?' she wheedled.

'Behave yourself, Simone,' he said. 'Remember. I know you very well. I have business—and it keeps you in bikinis. And yes, I have your birthday present and it'll have to wait for the party. In the meantime, I'm going to put something else on.'

'Do you have to?' She teased him, considering his hard-muscled body under her false lashes. Tanned, divine, but not quite as devoted as of late. Sometimes, she wondered if she loved him. Probably not, she thought, but they were good together. Jean-Luc was the faithful type and she didn't have to worry about him going off with someone else.

'Behave yourself,' he said. 'I'm going to the Villa des Anges and I shall be there all afternoon—working! Au revoir.' He looked at his watch and shook his head. 'You've exactly half an hour to get to your father's and no, you can't take the Ferrari, because I need it, but,' she could see he was relenting already, 'I'll drop you off, if you like.' He waited.

'No, thank you,' Simone yawned, 'I'll get a cab.'

'But a cab is not so fast, remember,' he replied, smiling.

'You sound just like my father. Goodbye,' she said, turning over in her deck chair.

She knew how to wind him up. In fact, she quite enjoyed it, which made up for his lack of attention and his absolute insistance on punctuality. She closed her eyes until she heard the roar of the Ferrari's engine.

She jumped up, knowing that François had been watching the byplay between them. She waved a limp hand and the swarthy young man, who desperately wanted to be her lover, came leaping down from the bridge. He was the recipient of one of Simone's most glorious smiles followed by a pretty pout which had earned Simone and her model figure a place on two of France's top fashion magazines.

Jean-Luc shook his head as he glanced back at his beloved yacht. *L'Hirondelle* seemed all that he had left of his old life, besides the Villa des Anges.

He could have bought a new yacht at any time, but he was determined to keep her. To him, she was vintage and meant childhood days, sailing in the Bay of Tropez and farther afield, cruising the Mediterranean with his father and sometimes his Tante Catherine. He didn't remember his mother. But now his aunt had left her old home and moved into an apartment in Monte Carlo, his father was dead and the family business was his concern—and a big headache.

Simone was too, but hers was a minor part compared with her father's. The business with Maurice Belleville had be settled, and soon. Then what Jean-Luc intended to do was not certain. Simone thought it was, but she'd have to think again. She believed she had his measure, but she hadn't. He felt he knew exactly what she was doing at that moment— probably driving François out of his mind.

Jean-Luc wasn't happy about his yacht master. Grimaud was Jean-Luc's home town and as one of the wealthiest inhabitants he knew most things that were going on there. He had his sources around the yachting bars and clubs. Even if François was stupid enough not to know to keep clear of his boss's girlfriend, he ought to have realised at least to keep better male company on his nights off.

Given his position, Jean-Luc had to be security conscious and if François was mixing with dodgy people then Jean-Luc would put up with it until they got back from his necessary trip to Monaco, because at least, the man was good at what he did sailing-wise. Jean-Luc liked to sail *L'Hirondelle* himself, but he was busy, so he needed François. However, if he didn't mend his ways, he'd be out of a job.

Jean-Luc slowed the Ferrari down and she rumbled in disgust. Eros was the newest of the line of Hilarie Ferraris and the family had tried them all. The name Eros was naff but it made him laugh. Ferrari owners tended to be over the top, it was expected. All his Ferraris had borne the name, which had suited his earlier indiscretions and playboy mentality.

Now he'd put that wildness behind him. Now, he was looking for one girl in his life, someone who would grow to know him and who had no preconceived notions of what he had been, who was interested in more than his financial worth. A woman who loved Jean-Luc for himself, a girl who had integrity, one he could settle down with—and it wouldn't be Simone, childhood playmate or not. She didn't know it yet, but even she must have an inkling that he wasn't that keen any more. He couldn't live the life she wanted. It would have to be an open relationship for her and an open marriage, because it was not in her nature to be faithful, even to a full wallet.

He could see the outcome. Their relationship would peter out eventually like most of his relationships with entirely unsuitable women like Simone. Ferrari owners were like that. *Perhaps I should grow up and buy a Lamborghini,* he thought, half-serious as he headed for the Villa des Anges.

He glanced at his Patek wrist watch. Like *L'Hirondelle,* it was part of his past. It had belonged to his father.

Not too long and he'd be home. He sighed. What would be waiting for him? A pile of letters. A deal of puzzles posed by the accountants he brought in and an unwelcome birthday party for Simone, which was the next horror on his calendar. She'd invited a cache of her best friends. He grimaced. It would

30

be anybody and everybody, even a top gossip magazine, but he'd put a stop to that. He hated publicity. *L'Hirondelle*'s salon could take around sixty-nine guests, but he told Simone she couldn't ask more than twenty. She'd actually sworn at him.

'Do as I say or buy your own yacht,' he'd said. He had to be hard sometimes because she drove him mad. He knew the present he had for her wouldn't be what she wanted, which was a diamond engagement ring, offered on one knee.

As he drove away from the yacht harbour, a black Mercedes pulled out of its parking space and dropped off a dark-suited man who made his way towards the yachts. Then it sped off and soon caught up with the Ferrari and followed it at a reasonable distance along the winding coast road towards Grimaud.

Jean-Luc was going fairly slowly which didn't suit Eros, which groaned through the gears. He smiled. The car was more suited to an owner who raced it on the Corniche, which he'd done pretty often. He now had too many other things to think about.

Finally, when he indicated towards the port, the Mercedes with its two sinister-looking occupants, turned right as well.

* * *

Lauren couldn't place where she was when

31

she woke. The shutters were rattling and the atmosphere was stifling. Then she remembered that Gary had tried to hit on her!

＊She turned over, churning all the possibilities in her stomach. It was going to be a hellish time. She had seen this coming and her reluctance to give up on what had seemed her dream job was why she was feeling like this now. Something had to give.

She'd never been indecisive, nor so torn. She turned over again, then throwing the covers aside, swung her slim, brown legs down to the cool floor. Marble—what else? Gary expected marble. Life with him would be good in financial terms. It would be exciting, but it would be on his terms not hers—and she suspected that one day he'd tire of her and go find a long-legged blonde. According to the photos she'd seen publicity wise, he preferred blondes anyway. Lauren didn't fit the bill. What they'd had in Venice had been pure excitement brought out by the beauty of the place.

She'd learned and it was probably partly her fault. Well, he knew now. He was as near to jumping her than he'd ever been a few hours ago and it scared her a little.

Good, old Paul, she thought as she stood under the shower and tried to wash her anxieties away. When she came out, swathed in one of the luxurious towels and with another wrapped around her head, she did feel better.

She'd made herself clear. She would stick the job out until the South of France was only a memory like all those other beautiful places.

'If he doesn't take the hint now—and if the worst comes to the worst—then I'll start looking around,' she said to herself.

It was very hot in the room. Streaks of light were forcing their way through the shutters urging her to get out there, to enjoy them. The impatient wind was making the white wooden slats rattle. The Mistral.

But what about romance? As far as she was concerned at the moment at least, it was dead.

'One day, Lauren,' she said out loud, sighing, 'One day, the whole lot will come along in one enormous package.'

Inexplicably she was thinking about the man she'd met at the stop off on the auto route. She remembered the sad look in those beautiful eyes. He had trouble too. *We all have troubles, Lauren,* a little voice said inside. At least we're having some good times in the middle of this awful recession. At least you have a job.

She was shocked when she looked at her watch; she'd been asleep a long time — and neither of them had disturbed her. She couldn't hear a sound. Maybe Gary and Paul had gone out. Paul definitely wouldn't be asleep; he hardly slept, like a man who needed none, but he was able to appear lazy. What a talent, she thought. Gary would be working for sure. He spent hours on the telephone to all corners of the world.

Lauren unpacked. She had learned to pack carefully as they might find themselves stopping over anywhere for a few hours and then travelling on.

In her job, she had to be prepared for Gary to say, 'Cocktail party. Smart. I'm meeting so and so . . .'

Lauren had a job where she had to be constantly ready. Maybe this one would be different. Gary was certainly in a big hurry and he was also pre-occupied with something or someone else. He'd taken a lot of messages on the way—and he hadn't discussed them with either her or Paul. It wasn't work. He'd said it was going to be a holiday and Gary didn't take holidays. Something was going on in Port Grimaud and he wanted to be part of the action. But she'd find out eventually—she always did. Except for Africa. She'd been properly excluded from that one. It had been something entirely Paul's and Gary's and Paul had not breathed a word about it either.

I don't like mysteries, Lauren thought, frowning at herself in the mirror as she put on her make-up. What was wrong with her?

After she'd dressed she felt more cheerful—and hungry. *I could do with*—she was imagining French food and now Lauren was dizzy for lack of it. As she didn't know where they were going, she'd put on a simple dress. Well, it looked simple, but it was Zara. The pretty espadrilles made up for her lack of height, about five-seven but the shoes made her taller. She needed to be to stand up to Gary!

Where the hell are they? she thought. *I hope we're going out to dinner tonight!* The emphasis was on *we;* she wasn't going without Paul, it would be too awkward. *Maybe Gary will give me my cards,* she thought whimsically. But he'd said he'd keep on trying. *Bad luck, Gary,* she thought.

With new resolve she opened the door and walked out into the living area. Paul was lying along a chaise longue under a wide open window, checking his camera. He looked remarkably smart for the daytime, except he'd forgotten to press the suit—it was creased white linen—and he looked hot.

'There must be an iron somewhere,' she said pointedly.

'I don't do those, but wow! Are we going somewhere?' He returned her look, his eyes on her dress.

'I could ask you that. White suit.'

'It's hot,' he said, 'and I have to look the part. This is the South of the France and I'm a top photographer.'

She laughed. 'I thought you were all dead in here,' she replied. 'It was so quiet. Where is he?' she, grimacing.

'Licking his wounds? No way. He's . . .' Paul shrugged. '. . . busy—in the only way Gary can

35

be.'

'What's it about, Paul? It doesn't sound like a holiday to me.'

'Contacts. At least, that's what I think. To change the subject. You look absolutely fantastic. Red suits you.'

'Thank you.' She gave him a twirl and the full skirt billowed. 'Don't do that when he comes in. You'll give him a heart attack.' They both fell about laughing then stopped.

Gary was standing at the door, looking at his most handsome. His linen suit wasn't creased, his hair was attractively floppy and if she hadn't known what he was like she could have fancied him, although she preferred dark-haired men. Oh, yes, thought Lauren, he's due somewhere.

'Did you sleep well?' asked Gary coolly. He didn't do hot.

'Like a log,' came the stock answer. 'Am I late for something?' Whatever he said, she intended to remain her usual self, except she felt strangely reckless, as though she didn't care any more about her job—or anything. She wanted to be out there—and free.

'It's hot out there, boss,' said Paul. He was turning over the pages of a magazine about cameras. Gary frowned.

'This place isn't air conditioned,' he remarked. He glanced at Lauren. 'Good choice, that dress. Nice colour. Paul's got some bread in. We'll eat later.'

'How much later,' asked Paul. 'Are we going out properly? Lauren's hungry, aren't you?'

'Yes, I am,' she said.

'There's some bread and cheese and wine. I'm waiting for a call,' replied Gary.

Paul got up and sighed. 'Shall we?' He indicated Lauren to sit down at the pretty table by the window.

She regarded Gary. *Why does he think he can treat us like this,* she thought, Then she knew she had to say something.

'I hope this isn't your way of paying me back for earlier, Gary. Starving us! Paul didn't upset you. It isn't his fault,' It was the only way to handle Gary, to challenge him. 'Well?'

'I don't know what you mean,' he replied.

'Well, I'm not going to put up with this. I only work for you. I'll go and find myself a restaurant. I was going out anyway.'

She could see Paul out of the corner of her eye. He was waiting for the outburst. She wished that he'd tell Gary what he thought of him, but he probably had more to lose than she did.

'If you do, you better take him. It can get rough here.' She hadn't been expecting that reply and sat down. Gary was looking at his phone again.

'This'll suit me fine, boss,' Paul said. He was staring at two bottles. 'Red or white?' Gary shrugged. 'Lauren?'

'She's waiting for an apology,' said Gary.

'I haven't done anything.' Paul retorted.

'Not you! Alright, Lauren, I'm sorry.' Gary said, then clammed up. At least he made her feel better.

'White, please.' She looked at Paul, who winked at her. 'And some more coffee?' She sat without saying anything. When Paul brought it over, she said, 'Thanks, Paul, that's good.'

'Maybe it'll help your temper,' said Gary.

The atmosphere was tense.

'This afternoon's not going to be good though,' muttered Paul, as he went back to the kitchen. 'If we're going out, let's go before you have too much on an empty stomach.'

Lauren raised her eyebrows, indicating Gary, who was still staring at the phone. It rang, he grabbed it and walked off.

'Why did we take this job, Paul?'

'For the cash.' He grinned. 'Feel better now you've taken him on, do you?'

'Not particularly. Why don't you stand up to him?'

'I've got mouths to feed,' the photographer replied grinning. He got up. 'Come on!' Paul urged.

'I can't come now until I know if he wants me or not. Remember, it's my job.'

'He won't,' said Paul.

She frowned at the response. 'How do you know?'

'Instinct. Men have them too, you know,

love.'

Then Gary returned, looking relaxed, his mood changed.

'Dinner?' she said.

'Something's come up.' He looked pleased. Yes, thought Lauren, this is the agenda I'm supposed to know nothing about.

'Will you need me?'

'I always need you, darling,' came the annoying reply. 'No, you go off and have fun with Paul. And, Lauren, I'm sorry—really. It won't happen again.'

'Credit card, boss,' said Paul, holding out his hand.

'The usual,' he replied. 'And have a great time. Oh, but you'll have to walk. I'm taking the Land Cruiser. Get a cab back.' He was already putting a file in his briefcase. 'Have fun, folks!' He threw Paul some keys, then came back and handed Lauren another key. 'The villa. I don't think it would be a good idea to be late. Stay safe.' Then he was gone.

'He's insufferable,' blurted Lauren.

'Think of the perks,' Paul said, drawing out the gold credit card. 'Where are we headed?'

She was slipping her small bag crosswise across her chest; she'd always been safety conscious. 'You mean where am I headed, don't you?'

'You heard what he said.'

'I don't need a minder, Paul. What were you going to do?' He tapped the camera. 'Well then, you do your thing and I'll do mine. I'm only going exploring . . . shops and things.'

'You better have this then.' He handed her the card. 'Go on, do some damage!'

'No, it'll give him the wrong idea. I'll use my own.'

'Take it. We'll meet at the Coq d'Or. It's a great restaurant.'

'Have you been here before?' She was surprised.

'No, I looked it up on the Web.' Paul was prepared for anything. He was like a big brother.

He pointed. 'It's at the top of that hill. You can't miss it. At the sign of the golden rooster. We'll meet there at six.'

'You're full of surprises, aren't you?' she said in a fond tone.

'Well, look who I work for.' He grinned. 'And don't talk to any strange men.' Paul was already getting his camera ready.

'Don't worry, I can look after myself. This isn't Barcelona,' she retorted and blew him a kiss.

As she began her way along the street, a man slipped out of the shadow of a doorway and began to follow her.

CHAPTER THREE

The red Ferrari was nosing its way along the narrow street when Jean-Luc saw the girl he'd met on the auto route. He couldn't fail to recognise her, which surprised him when he thought about it, as her jeans and top had been replaced by a delectable dress with a skirt that swung with her sexy walk.

As he was approaching, he drove especially slowly, savouring the sight. That she had been coming to Port Grimaud was certainly surprising. He didn't believe in Fate, if he had, he might have thought it so, but it was a pleasant coincidence.

He looked up from the low-slung sports car and smiled as he passed, knowing he could discover where she was staying. The Hilaries had their ways and means of finding out about anyone. He nodded, but as expected she didn't acknowledge him.

Lauren had heard the low whine of the powerful engine and watched as the Ferrari slunk off along the street. She could hardly believe it; it was the same man she'd met on the auto route. It must be Fate, she thought, seeing him again. That he should be here, of all places, was amazing.

Oh, don't be so stupid, she thought as the car disappeared. *How would you get to know him anyway? He's probably a millionaire.* She had met a few before at functions she'd attended with Gary, but they hadn't been in the least attractive, in spite of their bank balances.

She wondered if the Ferrari driver lived nearby. Maybe she'd meet him in town? She fantasised as to how that might happen and where they'd go, when her daydreams brought her out into another square, which was lined with souvenir shops.

The market Paul had mentioned was laid out under the spreading trees. The sun was low in the sky, bathing it all in orange gold. No-one seemed to be packing up as they did in England. Instead, the square was just coming alive. It was a riot of noise and colour, selling everything from monkeys to jewels. *That's illegal,* she thought, looking at the tiny animals. The stall holders looked mainly of African descent, probably Moroccans, and some of them were naked to the waist, sitting behind bells and bags spread out on the pavement.

As she walked past, they stretched and tried to catch her arm demanding attention. She shook her head and passed on. Dark girls were offering beautiful hand-made jewellery, some with wild flowers captured forever in glass pendants. Lauren bought herself a dark-red necklace of glass beads and a matching bracelet—they were a good match for her dress.

She sat down on an iron seat encircling a

tree and tried them on. Behind her rose cages of birds, finches and canaries and at her feet across the pavement were cages of rabbits and chickens. Lauren shuddered knowing for what fate the poor things were destined. The seller caught her eye and approached, but she shook her head and waved him away, wishing she could buy all of them and save them.

Several men passed her and smiled, but she looked away, got up and moved on, lost in her enjoyment of the market and oblivious of the two men following her now.

*　　　*　　　*

Jean-Luc parked Eros in the driveway of his villa at the very top of the street. He got out, still wondering whether he should go and look for her. If he was some lovestruck kid, he might have walked all around the town, but he had work to do, which wasn't a prospect he was looking forward to. Yet, all at once, the evening seemed a brighter prospect. He had lied about Simone's birthday present. Her expectations might be high but still she was going to get a diamond drop pendant he'd bought a few years ago. It had been meant for her, but he'd never given it to her. He'd ask Cecile, his housekeeper to wrap it.

Maybe he'd walk down the hill and bump into the girl. Then he shook his head at his stupidity. He wasn't in a movie.

43

He stood, fiddling with the car keys, wondering whether she'd be in the market place. He felt he was being dragged towards that possibility. She had seen him—and probably recognised him. Jean-Luc wasn't used to chasing girls any more.

You're behaving like an old man, he told himself, you're only twenty-five. Get down there and do something about it.

He locked the car and started down the hill towards the Coq d'Or. If it was Fate, then he would meet her again. Where were the two men she was with? They must have been crazy to let her out of their sight. He walked faster.

As for Simone . . . he shook his head. She would probably turn up at the villa soon. Her father was meeting some Englishman called Grey and she would have had enough of a business meeting in a couple of hours. She couldn't keep turning up at his place when things were so bad between them. He couldn't remember how long it had been since they slept together. He was soon going to ask her to move her stuff from her suite. He was ashamed of himself for putting the decision off and not making a clean break.

Simone seemed like a fixture who'd always been there—and he didn't need the stress. It wasn't only him; he knew she had another lover somewhere at the moment—and he couldn't have cared less. It gave him the right to do the same, but before this girl became stuck in his head, he hadn't bothered. He had too much anxiety in his business life.

The sign of the golden cockerel swung in the breeze. The Hilaries owned the place and as he was about to pass, he stopped on a sudden whim. Jean-Luc stared down the street. There was no sign of the girl—so he turned and walked into the restaurant.

The maître d' came hurrying forward. 'Monsieur Hilarie! What a pleasure! You would like a table?'

'Everything going well?' Jean-Luc looked round. He had never regretted buying the restaurant or employing Pierre to run it.

'Business is great this week,' smiled Pierre. 'So many tourists. Japanese and Germans.'

'Good,' said Jean-Luc glancing at the door, 'I was passing and, yes, I would like a special meal here tonight.'

'Your favourite? And you're bringing a guest, Monsieur?' Pierre's world-weary eyes sparkled. Monsieur Hilarie's special guests were always beautiful. Jean-Luc nodded. 'You would like the sea view,' Jean-Luc nodded. 'I'll reserve it at once. What time, Monsieur?'

'From now on . . . just keep that table free.'

'Oui, certainement.'

Jean-Luc was already heading for the door. He looked out. No sign. He could hear the market in the distance. Next door was one of the town's most exclusive boutiques which was incorporated with a small jewellers which he did not own. He'd not been in there before. What he bought for Simone came from Cartier's, which she preferred. The small, bearded man in a black suit who owned this shop was reputed to do good business only with Arabs. That evening, the stocky figure of the owner was standing by the door. He had no air of deference about him when he nodded at Jean-Luc. In the window, behind a meshed security glass, was a magnificent pearl necklace, milky white and mounted against a blue velvet backdrop. Jean-Luc liked them better than diamonds. He'd had his fill of those.

'The pearl necklace?' said the owner, sensing a sale.

'Yes, I like it,' he replied.

'For a beautiful mam'selle.' It was hardly a question. Jean-Luc shrugged. 'I understand, Monsieur Hilarie.'

Of course, he knows my name, thought Jean-Luc, following him inside. The jeweller took the pearls down from the window. Jean-Luc gave them a cursory look and nodded. He knew their price range from experience, but that was immaterial. The owner handed him the credit card machine, totally au fait with the foibles of the rich.

'Can you deliver them to my villa, please? Immediately.' The jeweller inclined his head. Jean-Luc didn't intend to walk round the town with pearls in his pocket.

46

'Thank you, Monsieur Hilarie.' The deal was done with no more questions.

Further down the street, he paused at the florists to buy red roses. In spite of her sixty years and great experience of rich clients, the owner had a wistful look on her face when she handed over the long-stemmed beauties to Monsieur Hilarie who seemed more handsome every time she saw him. She shrugged; red roses weren't usually his style.

Then he was off again, but he was unlucky. As he entered the market, Lauren left it and, with the same two men shadowing her, began her climb towards the sign of the golden cockerel. She felt that it would be better to check out the place where they were going to eat. Paul had his strengths, but choosing a suitable restaurant wasn't always one of them.

*   *   *

Jean-Luc paused, rather feeling disconsolate and somewhat foolish. What was he doing, running round the town looking for some unknown girl he'd seen on the auto route? She was probably married to the exceptionally rude Englishman. He got up again, had it in mind to ditch the roses, but relented, thinking he might put them in his den—he certainly wouldn't give them to Simone. They were red and meant something he didn't want to say to her.

47

He had bought the pearls on a whim and they would look so much better on someone who appreciated them. He fantasised about the girl wearing them, but there was no guarantee he would find her. He had bought them purely for the pleasure of it and to look at them from time to time. In that way, Jean-Luc was a collector.

He waited for few moments, then shook his head, annoyed with himself for behaving like a teenager, he turned again and made his way back up the long street towards his villa.

*　　*　　*

Lauren stood looking in the window of the Coq d'Or. Well, Paul, you haven't done too badly this time, she said to herself. In fact, you done good. But it looks exclusive. I'll bet it's all booked up.

The medieval restaurant was right at the very top of the street. It must have a marvellous view of the sea on the other side, she thought, deciding to investigate one of the tiniest alleyways running down the side of it. Just as Jean-Luc jogged up and through the villa gates, she turned into a tiny café halfway down, where she ordered a cup of coffee.

She wondered whether to phone Paul and let him know she'd had enough now as she looked at her watch. She could see the bay glittering and a marvellous yacht below, but the cobbled path looked dizzy and too rough for her sandals. Besides, she was still a bit tired from the long journey down.

Paying the bill, she re-traced her steps. There wasn't another way to go except down past the Coq d'Or again.

She reached the turning circle for vehicles at the top of the street when she noticed the gates of the glorious villa, hidden by the profusion of bushes. They opened up on to the circle itself, so she imagined all that was behind the villa was the shore. She loved looking at houses, but could only could glimpse it from the road—a paradise of pink stucco with a roof garden of palms. She'd loved to have gone beyond the bend in the drive and decided to take a peak, since there was no-one around.

She was rewarded with the sight of marvellous bougainvillea tumbling down the pink walls and the scent of roses filling the air. She gasped when she saw, under the great sturdy palms shading the white stones of the drive, the crouching shape of a red Ferrari.

She approached the car, almost on tiptoe. There was a small coat of arms emblazoned on the dazzling paintwork. 'Wow,' she murmured. 'I'll bet it's his.'

Inside on the passenger seat lay a pair of expensive driving gloves and a white silk scarf. The haughty blonde flashed into her memory. Probably his wife, was her first impression. Feeling a bit like a criminal, Lauren made for the gates and hurried down the street almost as far as the Coq d'Or.

Jean-Luc stood in the hall, looking at the door, he was still in a strange mood. He couldn't settle at all. He had a sudden urge to go out and again and look for her, but this time he'd go in Eros. Perhaps she was staying outside the town and walking back now? He hurried across the spacious hall to the front door and out to where the car was parked.

*   *   *

By that time, Lauren was already standing halfway down the hill, with her mobile in her hand.

'Hi, Paul, I'm up here at the top of the street near the Coq d'Or, It looks great but I don't know If we'd get in without a reservation . . . you'll still meet me here? You're sure? . . . Ok, I'll wait here.'

Then a man stepped out of a doorway down the road using his mobile. He was staring up at her. She closed her phone as he approached her, feeling guilty in case he'd seen her run out of the villa gates.

Then he started to sprint in her direction and she turned instinctively and ran up towards the turning circle with him behind her. A moment later, he'd grabbed her round the neck with one arm and brought her down.

Lauren screamed as her knees buckled, then

50

she felt a rough hand clamped over her mouth. Her mobile clattered to the floor and she dropped her bag, as she tried to pull away from his hands, but it was no use. Terrified, she struggled for breath, as he dragged her down towards a dark doorway. One of her sandals was torn from her feet as she struggled. She could hear a car's engine approaching! Then with one violent push, she managed to pull her head up and bit down on his hand.

'Help!' she screamed as she heard him swear. He had his hand over the face again. Kicking and struggling, she was still being dragged—until his grip relaxed and she twisted out of his grasp as he reeled backwards.

'Run! Back to the top. Through the gates!' a man shouted.

She stood dazed. Someone was grappling with her would-be kidnapper. The car's engine was getting louder. It was coming up the street.

'Into the villa!' the man shouted. 'Run!' She saw him dive at the man's legs, then she turned and limped as quickly as she could across the road and through the gates, then hid out of sight behind a great sweet-smelling bush, shivering all over. The smell of her attacker was all over her . . . garlic and smoke . . .

Jean-Luc was thrown off the man's body backwards, but the man had his hand near his waist and then a knife flashed out. Jean-Luc backed away, and the man lunged at him, again and again. Getting killed was more than he'd bargained for. He glanced behind him. He was nearly home. He had his hand on the remote control for the gates, which he kept in his pocket. He could see that the guy thought he had a knife too. If only he could get inside.

Then the man stopped, turned and ran towards the car that was almost on them and was yanked in, the door swinging as it screeched into the turning space.

By then Jean-Luc had pressed the remote control and sprinted through. He bent forward, coughing and panting. He couldn't believe he'd just been in a knife fight! The black Mercedes had screamed round by now and was off down the road. Jean-Luc had noted the number in his head, but he wasn't sure he had it right. The car was already round the corner. It was her they were after, not him.

Still panting, he looked round, feeling in his pocket for a pen. He needed to remember the number for the police. He ran over to the car, wrote it down, then turned. Where was she?

'Hello!' he called. 'They've gone.' No answer. 'It's alright,' he shouted. 'You're safe.'

Then he saw a movement behind a bush and rushed over. She was sitting on the ground, arms round her knees, head down. He touched her on the shoulder and she jumped, then looked up at him with frightened eyes. She was crying and shaking and there was blood on her mouth.

'Cherie,' he said. 'You're safe now.' He

knelt beside her.

'Thank you,' she said, wiping her mouth with her hand. 'Thank you for helping me.'

Then she burst into tears. He didn't know what else to do, so he put his arms round her and held her. She was trembling. He looked across his beautiful garden, dreading what would have happened if he hadn't given up looking for her and come home.

A few moments later Lauren disengaged herself from his arms and reached out to take off her remaining sandal.

'Thank you again,' she said, grimacing. She shook her head. 'I lost my shoe . . . my bag . . . my phone.'

Jean-Luc let her go, stood up and held out his hands. She started to get up and winced. 'Oh!'

'I'll call the doctor,' he said.

'Who were they?'

'Muggers?' he replied and shook his head. He didn't really mean it; pickpocketing round the market area was a problem, but kidnapping with violence was something else and he'd never come across it here. She must have something they wanted.

'But why try to drag me in a car?' Her voice shook. 'I haven't got anything,' she began. Then thought of Gary's gold card. 'Oh,' she said, 'I have to phone the bank—my credit card.'

'Just make your way slowly to the house

and I'll go and look for your bag. Maybe they weren't after that.'

She stared at him, puzzled. 'What else would they be after? I'm coming to help you,' she said.

'You stay there,' he commanded. She disobeyed him and limped back towards the gates. He was down the street a little towards the doorway into which she'd been grabbed.

'It's here,' he shouted. 'Your bag.' He was sure now that this wasn't a mugging. Her mobile phone was still lying in the gutter. 'And your phone.' He picked it up, looking warily behind him all the time.

She was still standing there. 'Oh, thank you,' she said.

'Come on,' he said. 'Let's go inside and sort you out, then we'll get on to the police.' He was glad when she nodded in agreement. If she was willing to call the police, then she couldn't have anything to hide.

A man in a white suit emerged from a doorway further down. He had a camera slung over his back and he cursed out loud. He should have stuck closer to her, then the whole fiasco wouldn't have happened, but it was too late now. The damage was done and the Frenchman had saved the day. All he could do now was to ring her. He looked at his watch. He'd give her five minutes. And he had to get the story straight for Gary.

*   *   *

'I'm feeling better now,' she said, as they limped towards the house together.

'Well, you don't look it,' he quipped. 'And I didn't do my shirt any good either.' He lifted his arm and it came apart.

'And my shoes were new.' She looked at her bare feet with regret. He was carrying the remaining shoe. 'I think we'll have to throw that one away. My bag?'

He gave it to her. 'Don't search it now. Come on.'

'But my phone?'

'Here you are.' He handed it over. 'But I don't know if it still works.' She put it to her ear and nodded, then closed it.

'But what did they want?' It was all so horrible. One minute I was walking down and the next, he just caught hold of me.'

'I think he must have been following you, mam'selle . . . .?'

'I'm Lauren. Lauren James,' she said as they reached the house steps. The door was open and they faced each other.

'Jean-Luc Hilarie.' It seemed ridiculous to shake hands, so he just laid his hand on her arm.

'Thank you so much,' she said. 'Are you hurt? You might have been killed.'

'I don't think so.' He didn't mention the knife. 'I think it was only you they wanted.'

'But why?'

'I don't know, mam'selle, but they meant it.'

She shook her head. 'I don't understand. I must check everything's there.'

'Inside first.' he said. 'You need to sit down.'

A few seconds later, Lauren was entering a fine hall with a white marble floor and a broad staircase curving up to a higher level. Minimalistic was her first impression as a tall plinth faced her. On the top was the statue of an angel. Its gleaming white wings stood out against the dark coolness of the hall. Around the wide floor were scattered a quantity of bright coloured rugs with flowers and modern patterns adding to the whole Mediterranean feel. He caught her glance.

'Welcome to the Villa des Anges—there's only one angel inside.' He indicated the statue.

The whimsical joke was lost on her as she closed her eyes for a moment, hoping she wasn't going to faint. Of course, she hadn't had anything to eat either.

'You're very pale, Lauren,' he said. 'Come. I'm forgetting myself.' With his arm around her, he led her into a comfortably-furnished room, high-ceilinged but much less imposing than the hall, with subtle grey furniture and a matching modern desk facing the window, a computer on its surface.

He led her to a deep armchair and she sank into it. Then he strode out of the door and shouted something.

All she could think of at that moment was Gary—he'd go crazy—and Paul. She looked at her watch and was horrified—the glass was broken—but she knew it was past the time to meet him. She needed to go, but she didn't feel well, which was a sensation fairly unknown to Lauren.

Jean-Luc returned just as her mobile rang.

'Should I . . .?' asked Jean-Luc, indicating that he should leave. She shook her head as he stood beside her, curious to know who was calling.

'Paul? Paul!' she said, her voice wobbling. 'I think I've just been mugged.'

Of course, thought Jean-Luc, one of the Englishmen.

'I'll call the police,' he said, walking away. He took out his phone and was soon speaking in rapid French. By then, Lauren was beginning to feel better. Paul said he'd make a decision as to whether to tell Gary, adding he might cover for her instead or at least make it not bad as it seemed. Then he'd promised to come and fetch her as soon as he could.

Jean-Luc snapped his phone shut. The last thing he wanted was the police arriving at his home. 'I told them when you're feeling better we'll go down to the gendarmerie, but in light of what has happened I wouldn't be surprised if they turn up here.'

'Thanks so much.' Now she almost couldn't believe any of it had happened and as for

57

being saved by him . . .

'Feeling better? I'm glad I was nearby. I'd just been out.' This wasn't the time to tell her where. He wondered what she'd say if he did. She'd probably be scared stiff.

'You speak really good English.'

'I've lived in London. Business.'

'I see.'

She'd thought he was a playboy, she thought and then realised that his shirt arm had been torn right across. He caught her looking and she smiled.

'I must look awful.' She looked down at her dress. Damn—a couple of hundred had disappeared in five minutes. She couldn't wear this again—and what about her shoes!

'Not at all,' he said gallantly. 'I've taken the liberty . . . Ah.' He turned. A pleasant-looking middle-aged woman in a black dress was coming in with a tray.

Definitely not his mother, thought Lauren.

'My housekeeper,' he said on cue. 'Thank you, Cecile.' She put the tray down on the coffee table.

'Shall I pour, sir?'

'No, no,' he waved her away. She seemed entirely oblivious of his guest.

'Very good, sir.'

Jean-Luc turned to Lauren.

'Coffee . . . Sugar? Or milk?' He grimaced. 'I told you I'd lived in England.'

She smiled; she liked men with a sense of

58

humour.

'White—with one sugar.'

He grinned back. 'Shall I pour?'

She nodded and he did so. The right arm of his shirt was now hanging off, revealing his bicep. *That shirt probably cost more than my dress,* thought Lauren.

'Then, perhaps, the smallest brandy?' he added.

'Coffee, yes, but no thanks to brandy. I had a glass of wine before I came out. I don't really drink spirits.'

'Ah,' he said. 'I think we should set about getting you into some new clothes.' He was looking at her dress.

'Oh, I'm not far away. Gary has hired a villa near the harbour and Paul is coming to fetch me.' She didn't want to move.

'Gary?' he said.

'Yes, my employer. I'm his personal assistant.'

Jean-Luc felt relieved and replied, 'And Paul?' He handed her the coffee.

'Oh, Paul . . .' She smiled. Disappointment hit him at her evident pleasure this Paul's name gave her. 'Paul. He's lovely. He works with me.'

'I see.'

She sipped her coffee and she thought, Damn him! He should have been looking after me.

'He doesn't have to come. I can take you

back. Remember, we have to stop at the police station.'

'Gary will go crazy. Paul won't mind coming.'

'Here?'

'Do you mind? He doesn't want to let Gary know what happened. Neither do I.'

'You still look pale,' said Jean-Luc. 'Why don't you give him another ring and tell him he doesn't have to. I'll take you home.'

It was better than Lauren had hoped for. She really wanted to get to know this man better. They were looking at each other in what they both knew was undeniable mutual attraction, but the whole thing was ridiculous—he had a wife or a girlfriend.

Lauren had noted the little touches that only a woman could give a house, but of course, she was hoping it might be the housekeeper. Then she jettisoned the thought. She had no doubt such an attractive guy had a woman in tow, probably the girl they'd seen at the stop off.

At that moment, everything seemed trivial and she felt very scared, which was so much out of character. Who would have tried to drag her into a car like that, and what for? It was horrible, but she knew at that moment, this is where she wanted to be as she felt very safe with Jean-Paul.

'I couldn't put you to the trouble of taking me back,' her eyes were appealing. He

60

smiled and shook his head. She hesitated then withdrew her phone. Paul's number was engaged and she left him a message,

'Paul? Don't come to fetch me. Mr Hilarie is arranging to bring me back. We have to stop off at the gendarmerie, but tell Gary not to worry.'

'Is it ok?' Jean-Luc asked.

'He'll be cool about it and square it with Gary.'

'Good, then I'll get Cecile on the case.' He was beginning to dislike this Paul, whom she trusted so much.

'The case?'

'New clothes. We need to get you out of that dress—it's torn the back.' He raised his eyebrows.

'No!' she tried to look. 'I thought it was just dirty.'

'That's why I thought you'd like something else to put on.'

'I couldn't possibly impose. I'll change when I get back.'

'Have I offended you?' asked Jean-Luc. 'Maybe I shouldn't have said anything, but . . .'

'Oh no, you should have.'

'But you must have shoes. Lauren, may I say something? I'm not taking advantage here, I'm offering a dress, not anything else . . .' He was determined to keep her as long as he could, whereas he couldn't wait to get rid of Simone, who treated the place like her own. In fact,

61

she thought it was hers by right. But he wasn't having that either. He'd come to his senses.

'Jean-Luc, may I say something?' She looked embarrassed.

'Oui, mam'selle?'

'Well, perhaps some sandals and . . . maybe a dress . . . You've been so kind. What you did for me, tackling that awful man. That wouldn't have happened in London. Most people ignore muggings, because they're too scared to interfere.'

'It's the same here too, Lauren,' He pronounced her name in a heavenly French way. 'But I was trained in rugby with the local team. It was good practice.'

He looked so whimsical that she had to laugh. He joined in.

'Now, I'll just have a word with Cecile.'

Jean-Luc charged off in case he said the wrong thing. His earlier doubts were disappearing. How could she be mixed up with something that someone would be willing to use a knife for? She couldn't be guilty of any crime—and he was going to tell the police exactly that.

Lauren looked round the room and tried to relax. The geometric designs in the wide hall were reflected in the rugs, but the neutral tones and the grey furnishings gave the room a masculine feel. The bookcases on the wall were dark and some of the books were interspersed with porcelain. It was a masculine room but there were unmistakable feminine touches.

He returned. 'I've asked Cecile to lay out a couple of things for you. She has a good eye for what suits. Would you like to go and see?' he indicated the door. She tried to move and realised she was aching. 'Oh, but you've been hurt,' he said.

'Not really, I suppose it was when he was dragging me, although he hurt my lip with his hand. I'm afraid I bit him!'

'Wow!' he said. 'I'm sure the police will be looking for them. I gave a description, but they'll probably want to talk to you.'

'I couldn't really let this one go, I suppose?'

'Definitely not,' he replied looking at her. 'It's bad for the tourist trade.'

They laughed together. He was so easy to get on with and not in the least like Gary. Lauren thought of him—at this present moment he'll be giving Paul hell, she thought.

'Now, shall we?' Jean-Luc stretched out his hand and pulled her up. Even in her present state, she couldn't help noticing his hands were strong and firm. He continued, 'And then afterwards, we'll decide what to do next. I hope you don't need to hurry off. Where were you headed when it happened?'

'I was thinking of going down to the shore.'

'The beach is all rocks there. I have a private beach, at the bottom of the garden. Maybe you'd like to come and see? But only when you feel better.'

'I'll really have to get back. I have to work.'

'Then perhaps you would have dinner with me this evening?'

She didn't need a pair of appealing brown eyes to remind her she hadn't eaten properly for ages.

'Yes, I'd like that,' she replied. 'Paul and I were going to dinner together as Gary had a business meeting. Somebody called Belleville. Perhaps you know him?' He didn't speak. 'We were going to go to that restaurant near to where it happened.'

'The Coq d'Or? That's a coincidence. I'm booked in there myself for this evening.'

'Really? Then I'd love to. But I have to go back first.'

'Let's talk about that afterwards. Please come.' They walked across to the door.

'This is a lovely house,' she said.

'Yes, it's been in my family a very long time. Once I thought I would sell it, but now I've changed my mind.'

'Don't sell it,' she said, walking through the door into the hall. 'You're sure to regret it.' Everything is so beautiful here, she thought. He indicated the stairs.

'Cecile is waiting for you. Up to the landing, first door on the left in the corner. There is an en suite.'

'Thank you again.'

He shrugged in that familiar Gallic way.

She went up the stairs, not looking behind, but she could feel his eyes burning her back. The landing was spacious and the house must have about nine bedrooms on this floor.

She didn't know whether to knock, but the moment she reached the door, Cecile stepped out.

'Mam'selle. I have laid out some things which I think might suit. If you are not happy, then please ring for me. I was not sure about shoes, but the first cabinet is devoted to those. Please take what you wish.'

'Have you worked here for a long time?' asked Lauren.

'Twenty years and I have been very happy.' Her broken English was thick with emotion. She stood aside. A second later, Lauren was standing in a room which was unmistakably feminine. She sensed the occupant had extremely expensive taste. That figures, she thought. A huge vase of flowers stood beneath a table in front of the open window. Whoever owned the bedroom had no desire to lean out and breath in the scent of the roses outside.

The flowers were exotic, orchids and lilies that Lauren didn't recognise, all placed stylishly in cascading greenery. *Maybe it's a bouquet he's given her,* thought Lauren. No formal wardrobes could be seen except several antique armoires with curtains under the glass. Then she realised why. There was a dressing room adjacent—a walk-in wardrobe!

The bed was king-size with ornate caned ends in a softer grey as in the room below, the dove colour complementing the wall behind the bed, while all other walls were pure white.

She had stayed in luxurious hotels on her travels with Gary, but this was the ultimate home. On the high pristine bed lay three dresses, one white, one black and a very pretty modern silk print, with a full skirt like hers. She went over and picked up the black sheath first, feeling a bit like Goldilocks. For the evening and off the shoulder. It was labelled Dior.

'What else?' she said. Her eyes flicked at the label. Size 10.

The white was glorious, sultry, same label. Just right for getting mugged in! She thought wryly.

However the sprigged silk's skirt was voluminous, a modern swirl of exotic print and the designer was ultra-modern too. Who did they belong to? She was pretty sure none of them had ever been worn. Beside them lay an exquisitely embroidered robe and on a table beside was a pile of fluffy white towels. Seated, she could see the door of the en suite bathroom was ajar.

She took off her own dress. It made her feel sick—the man had dragged her along so roughly that he had caused the bodice to part from the skirt! It was ruined. In any case she didn't want to wear it ever again, nor to think about why they wanted her. Her grandma had always talked about the white slave trade. She'd thought it was ludicrous, but she'd seen a programme which had dealt with just that. It was horrible!

Then her eyes caught sight of the dressing table and she went over. On the glass that protected the wood had been laid accessories; matching jewellery, bracelets, pendants, necklaces. None were paste. Lauren sat on the chair in front of the mirror. She hadn't realised she looked so awful. She leaned her elbows on the table, feeling exhausted and overwhelmed. The she got up, feeling weary and made for the bathroom.

It was unbelievable. Twin porcelain basins built into a marble shelf, a linen vanity unit in the same grey with a black marble top; a tall cabinet with perfectly-ordered white towels and a hanging rail. On the high windowsill stood several fragrance diffusers with their sticks and candles in multi-coloured holders. Nothing was in short supply, all reflecting that splash of colour that seemed a motif throughout the house, giving it an exotic feel. The deep bath stood alone on curved feet and most surprising of all was a waterproof television fixed into the wall.

'Wow!' She looked at the bath longingly. She needed to wash away the smell of her attacker which hung around ominously, reminding her of what had happened earlier.

She was surprised there was no shower, but all at once she noticed a glazed recess in the wall. Looking through the sliding door, was a spacious wet room.

A quarter of an hour later Lauren, wrapped in a great fluffy towel around her body returned to the bedroom.

She decided to look in the walk-in wardrobe for shoes and gasped; she only seen such an array of designer gear in shops.

'The girl has everything,' she gasped. Her eye caught sight of a cabinet with the door slightly open.

'Shoes,' she breathed. She owned a few pairs herself, but there were at least a hundred here. She turned them over—all designer names.

'I can't wear her Jimmy Choos,' she murmured to herself, but she had no option. Each pair was more expensive than the other and—she couldn't believe it—they were all her size. She took the plainest pair she could find, the only concession being a peep-toe.

When she'd finished dressing, she decided she wouldn't wear her watch, seeing as it had been cracked.

Cecile had provided a bag into which she put her torn dress and ruined shoes. Maybe the police will want to look at them, she thought, then why would they? It's not as if it had been a murder or anything.

Then all of a sudden she had to sit down

on the bed again; the thought had made her wobble. It could have so easily been a murder—and not only hers. They might have killed Jean-Luc. He'd been so brave. The whole thing welled up in her mind and she had to pick up a delicately-scented tissue and dab her eyes.

* 'Phew,' she said, getting up and surveying her choice in the mirror. She had agonised over which dress to wear to go to dinner with him but she had decided against the white or the black. She wouldn't see herself wearing those. She doubted she would have been over-dressed in the Coq d'Or, but she had been conservative and had chosen the pretty silk.

Lauren grimaced when she thought of what the dress's owner might have said if they'd met!

She'd managed to tame her curls with her brush and felt a lot better now. Her anxiety regarding Gary's reception of the news had almost faded at the thought of going out with Jean-Luc. She owed him after saving her. Maybe Paul will keep his mouth shut, she thought, but then, the police might turn up, so he has to know. She closed the door behind her and walked across the landing, then paused.

Jean-Luc must have heard her because he was waiting at the bottom of the staircase. He'd changed into a perfectly-tailored sports jacket, open-necked shirt and chinos. She was relieved that she had worn the silk not the formal. He was looking as only extremely handsome guys do—adorable—that's until you get to know them, thought Lauren as she walked down the stairs. But he ticks all the boxes at present and, as I'm here, I'm going to enjoy it. She could see by the admiring look in his eyes that he approved of her choice.

'Thank you for the use of the bedroom,' she said. 'I didn't know what I should do with my old clothes. I'll get this laundered and then return it.'

'We will present this to the police,' he said, taking the carrier bag. She nodded.

'No calls?' he asked.

'No. Gary either hasn't come back or he must be satisfied with Paul's explanation.' Jean-Luc didn't answer. He would never understand the Englishman's attitude.

'Good, then if you're not feeling too tired, would you like to see my garden first? I am no gardener, but I have two. I only look.' His shrug plus the ashamed look made Lauren laugh.

'I'd love to see the garden.'

'And perhaps we could look at the beach?'

'That would be great.'

She was beginning to relax, but inside she kept asking herself why she'd been attacked. It all seemed like a nasty dream now, but would she feel safe again?

Jean-Luc looked relaxed as well as they

walked along chatting, stopping here and there to admire the flowers.

They went down a flight of white steps into a symmetrical Italian garden. Lauren knew it was classical Italian because there had been one at her school. Its lovely box hedges were perfectly trimmed and its ordered paths were paved with white gravel. At the end was a mock temple.

'It's lovely,' said Lauren.

'I call it my Petit Trianon,' he replied. 'Like the one at Versailles.' Lauren lifted her eyebrows. 'Facetious I know, but Marie Antoinette happens to be a favourite of mine.'

That figures thought Lauren, he's an aristocrat!

'I remember,' she said. 'We were in Paris some time ago and Paul and I managed to get in a visit. He's a very keen photographer.'

The last thing Jean-Luc wanted to talk about was Paul. 'I travel a great deal too, but I always come back here, to the Villa des Anges.'

'You have neighbours,' she asked. She could see another house at the end of the trees. 'Who lives there?'

'Maurice Belleville.'

'What a coincidence! That's where Gary's gone tonight,' she said—and stopped.

'Do you want to make a run for it?' asked Jean-Luc. He was joking, but his eyes were serious. 'I confess that I know he was meeting a travel writer this evening.'

'And a lot else, too, I believe,' replied Lauren.

'Really?' Jean-Luc was very interested now.

'Global business, but I only handle the book side. I don't know much about his other businesses. They're very complex. Gary Grey & Co are a well-known organisation.'

Jean-Luc's eyes were both intent and caressing. He wanted to take her on face value, but he'd had too many disappointments in the past.

Lauren sensed a different kind of attention from Jean-Luc and was about to respond when the moment was broken with a shrill bark, followed by three Pekinese bounding along the path.

Jean-Luc's expression had changed. Coming across the garden was a girl with a wonderful tan wearing a low-cut couture dress, its vivid silk clinging to her wonderful figure. The woman who'd been driving the Ferrari was staring at Lauren with undisguised hostility.

'Simone? I'm entertaining, too. This is Lauren James from London . . . Lauren, Simone Belleville.'

Lauren didn't betray shock or surprise, only smiled and extended her hand.

The girl ignored it, only bending to clip a golden chain on the three troublesome little dogs who had been cavorting around them. As she straightened from her task she was staring at Lauren's dress under her lashes, but then she looked away.

She must be seething, thought Lauren, seeing me in her clothes—if they are hers!

'Do you like them, Miss James?'

'Pardon?' Lauren was taken aback.

'The dogs.'

'Oh, I don't know much about Pekes,' she said, trying to regain her composure. Miss Belleville was not going to get the better of her. Lauren could be hard as well if need be.

'Jean-Luc is extremely fond of picking up tourists and showing them around our gardens,' Simone quipped. 'Has he shown you our beach, our pool, our horses? You must have shown her the horses, darling?

'Please go away, Simone,' he said sharply, surprising Lauren. 'Lauren isn't a tourist, she's one of Mr Grey's party.'

Simone's eyes narrowed. 'Why isn't she over at ours then?'

'Simone, you're insufferable. I do apologise, Lauren. Occasionally she behaves as if she owns me. We have known each other a very long time and . . .' his eyes were very angry, '. . . and I am always telling her she is highly-strung and extremely spoiled.' They regarded each other.

Lauren looked away. If they were going to have a row she didn't want to be there, so she walked off along the path. She could still hear Simone's shrill voice and then he was hurrying after her shortly.

'Please stop,' he said. She turned, just in time to see Simone flouncing off in the direction she'd come from, preceded by the yapping Pekinese.

'Forgive me?' he said. 'What you just heard was unforgivable. Don't let's talk about it. No-one owns me, Lauren, you see. I am not that lucky.'

She didn't know how to answer. 'I've told Simone to let Mr Grey know you are here. And she will.'

Lauren didn't know how to answer.

*   *   *

They spent the next couple of hours having a fabulous time, making her almost forget what had happened. Jean-Luc was a marvellous host and the villa was enormous in its surprises.

He didn't mention the police again, nor did he tell her anything about Simone. He had a way of making a girl seem particularly special and Lauren couldn't put it all down to Gallic charm. His hospitality was overwhelming.

She hadn't been prepared for what happened next.

Lauren was sitting in the plush garden suite with a drink and nibbles wondering how long it would be before they went to dinner, when she saw Gary approaching with Simone.

'Oh, dear,' she said, putting her drink down.

Jean-Luc was on his feet. Gary was tall, but Jean-Luc was taller by a head.

'Hello, Gary,' she said as he came up. He didn't reply, but she knew all his expressions and this was a bad one.

'Mr Grey.' Jean-Luc's voice was as smooth as his liqueur. 'Gary has come to fetch his employee,' said Simone sharply and Lauren winced.

'Did you have a good meeting?' she asked, hoping he wasn't going to be too rude. He might pay her, but he certainly didn't own her and he had given them the night off. He still hadn't spoken to Jean-Luc. His manners were as bad as his temper! There was no sign of Paul.

'Yes, I learned a lot about the French,' was the insulting answer. 'Are you ready?'

'This is Jean-Luc Hilarie and you need to say thank you to him. He got me out of a very difficult and frightening situation.'

Jean-Luc was frowning. 'You will learn, Mr Grey, that it's not the custom in France to turn up uninvited.'

'I get it, Monsieur Hilarie,' he said. 'I don't know what you've been up to, Lauren, but you can tell me all about it when we get back to our hotel.'

'You gave me the night off,' she said.

Gary turned to Jean-Luc. 'Doubtless you've been entertaining her very well, but I need her. Where's your bag?'

Lauren looked at Jean-Luc, then at Gary. No way, boss or not, that he was going to treat her like a piece of furniture.

'I think you should leave,' said Jean-Luc.

Lauren interposed. 'I'm not ready yet, Gary,' she said.

He looked at both of them. 'How will you get home?' he said.

'I shall be delighted to bring her,' replied Jean-Luc, 'When she's ready.'

Simone was glaring at Jean-Luc. *Serve them both right for their arrogance,* thought Lauren. She'd have to face she might have talked herself out of her job. She had never seen Gary at a loss for words. Even his face was red.

'Right,' he said. 'I'll go then.' He directed a curt nod to Jean-Luc and turned.

Simone shot a poisonous glance towards Lauren. 'I'll show you out,' she said to Gary.

'My chauffeur will take you to your vehicle,' Jean-Luc added.

'No thanks. I'd like a word with Lauren in private, before I go,' snorted Gary.

'Do you want to?' Jean-Luc asked Lauren directly.

'It's fine. He doesn't scare me,' she muttered.

Jean-Luc withdrew.

'What the hell are you doing here?' asked Gary.

'Having a drink,' replied Lauren calmly.

'I mean how did you get here? How do you

know him?'

'I was out walking and we met by accident.'

'I told Paul to look after you.'

'I'm not a child, Gary.' Her mind was computing. So Paul hadn't told him—which meant there could be a ticklish problem with the police.

'I don't trust him,' said Gary. 'He might be a rapist or something.' She could see by his face he really meant it.

'Get real,' she said. 'Just go home and I'll be back later. He's treating me to dinner.' She shook head. 'Just go, please. You've behaved abominably.'

'You know why.'

'I don't want to hear it,' she said, 'Goodbye, Gary. I'll see you in the morning.'

'The morning!' he repeated.

'Go away, Gary,' she said.

She looked towards Jean-Luc, but Simone came up to Lauren and hissed, 'And keep the bloody dress. I didn't want it anyway. It looks cheap on you.'

Lauren grimaced. Simone caught up with Gary and slipping a hand under his arm, the two of them walked off.

Jean-Luc came up to her. 'Alright? Doesn't he have a mobile phone?' Jean-Luc asked Lauren. She didn't catch on. 'Why didn't Grey ring? Or am I missing something here?'

'That was so childish,' she said. 'Simone told him and he thought he'd fetch me, but nobody owns me either.'

Lauren looked at Jean-Luc, then they both began to laugh.

'I don't know what came over me. I was awfully rude to him. I'll probably get the sack.' She paused. 'I owe you an explanation. I want to apologise for his rudeness. He . . .'

'There is something between you.'

'Whatever it was, it's over, and it was just . . .'

Why am I telling someone I've only just met that I haven't slept with my boss, Lauren thought. But somehow, it seemed very important.

'I was flattered when he gave me the job, but it hasn't turned out that way. Things have become . . . awkward. I've put a stop to it and he doesn't like it, that's all. I'm sorry.'

'Don't be,' he said. 'Let's enjoy each other's company and as the English say, I think, we are both in the same boat.'

'Are we?'

Her heart lifted. So he wasn't in love with Simone, although looking at the two of them together she wasn't surprised.

'I can safely say yes. We all make mistakes.'

A moment later, his phone rang. 'Excuse me.'

She nodded as he had a short conversation.

'The police,' he said after he hung up.

'Do they want to speak to me?'

'They want to come here. It would be

78

unwise to refuse. Are you ready?' His face was serious.

'Of course, if you don't mind, but I didn't expect any of this.'

The whole horrid experience overwhelmed her again. She had been hoping Gary wouldn't find out, but that hope was fading.

He shook his head. 'I expected it. Just to warn you, the police here are officious. I mean—they're not the friendly type. That's the French way.'

'Sounds awful,' she grimaced.

'Remember you're not on your own. If needed, I have friends in high places. I would have preferred we went down there, but they had other ideas, which means they're taking this very seriously, which they should be.'

'Thanks for the warning, Jean-Luc,' she said, 'But why should I worry, I've nothing to hide.'

CHAPTER FOUR

The police were in plain clothes. There were two of them, a man, who introduced himself as Inspector Etienne and a woman, who looked like his sergeant. Throughout the interview, Lauren had the impression that Jean-Luc was on edge and although they treated him with deference, she could see he found the whole thing embarrassing.

Lauren had to go through the usual kind of explanation; why she was in Grimaud, where she came from, what was her business. Jean-Luc had asked if she wanted him to be there at that point, but she had nothing to hide. She handed over the bag with her dress in case they needed evidence.

'But nothing's been stolen,' she said. 'I can't imagine what they wanted with me.'

'That's what we would like to find out, mam'selle,' the inspector said. 'And we will. You were carrying no valuables?'

'Only my mobile and personal documents—and of course a credit card,' she replied.

'Your business in being in town this afternoon?' He waited.

'I was sightseeing and then we were going to have dinner at the Coq d'Or.' She saw Jean-Luc raise his eyebrows. 'I'm Mr Grey's personal assistant and I really don't want him involved. He knows nothing about this.'

'He was actually having a meeting with Mr Belleville at the time,' interposed Jean-Luc.

'Maurice Belleville,' the inspector repeated.

'Yes.'

'Your business associate, Mr Hilarie?' Jean-Luc nodded.

This was news to Lauren!

'I assume then, that Mam'selle James was visiting you because . . .?' the inspector asked.

'Oh, but I wasn't visiting him. I was out for a

80

walk and we—that is, Paul and I—were going to meet for dinner. We only arrived earlier in the day.'

'Paul?' The inspector looked at her with an expression that made Lauren feel very uncomfortable.

'He's—'

The inspector cut her short. 'You can explain about Paul in a moment. Let's go back to the assault.'

That's what it was—not a mugging, she thought.

The inspector continued. 'Then it was lucky that Monsieur Hilarie was on hand to come to your aid?'

Lauren had the sudden feeling they didn't believe a word.

'I don't know where this is leading, inspector,' said Jean-Luc. 'This is the first time I've made Miss James's acquaintance.'

At that moment, he was feeling very uncomfortable and annoyed. The police had investigated his father's untimely death, which had been put down to natural causes. However, he had always had the feeling that someone was holding something back. He didn't like the way they were acting, as if they were insinuating some connection between him the Englishman and Belleville.

'I am only happy to say that if I hadn't been in my garden at the time of the attack, you might have had a missing tourist case on your

81

hands,' he snapped. 'Did you trace the car?'

Lauren started. He hadn't told her he'd taken the number.

'They were false plates,' said the inspector, staring hard at both of them. 'We made a thorough search on our database and checked with Interpol. Maybe—you mistook the number?'

'Maybe I did,' he said, 'Since I had to run for my life when the man pulled a knife on me!'

'Interpol?' asked Lauren, confused.

'You are a foreign national, Miss James.' The police woman spoke for the first time. 'It's normal practice in this case.'

'But I haven't done anything wrong.'

'We have to inquiries to pursue. This is a serious matter. It was best to come and inform you of the position. Naturally, we need to keep in touch with you. Your passport, please.'

'My passport?'

'I'm sorry, mamselle, but this is standard practice.'

Lauren was about to remonstrate when Jean-Luc shook his head at her.

'We shall keep it for as short a time as possible until we have done our checks. Please.' The woman held out her hand while Lauren rummaged in her bag.

'Here,' she said, feeling shaken.

'Will you be leaving Grimaud soon?' she asked.

'No, Gary—I mean Mr Grey—has taken the villa for two months,' Lauren replied.

'Address?'

'I don't know.' They looked at her and she added defensively, 'We only arrived this morning.'

'And you're Mr Grey's personal assistant?' Disbelief was written all over her face.

'Mr Grey booked the villa. He does sometimes. He said it was business combined with a holiday. It's quite normal for him. It was meant to be a surprise for us.'

All three of them were staring at her now.

'Us?'

'Yes, the other man with us, Paul—Gary's photographer. He and I were going to dinner.'

'Have you his address?'

'He's staying with us. He and Gary work together all the time. Why do you want to know all this?'

They ignored the question.

'Very well, mam'selle. Where exactly is this surprise villa?' Lauren winced. 'The location. Can you describe it?'

'Of course. It's in the bridge by the square.' She gave them directions. 'Will you be calling on Gary?'

'That won't be necessary. We'll check with the letting agent, but it might come to that and we'd like you to stay in touch.'

'I haven't much option without my passport,' said Lauren. Jean-Luc looked at her anxiously and she took the hint.

'We're very sorry that this has happened here in Grimaud, Miss James.'

You certainly sound sorry—not! thought Lauren.

The inspector indicated the bag.

'Naturellement, we shall be examining this to see if it might render up some clues on your attacker. Mr Hilarie,' he turned to Jean-Luc, 'You will be hearing from us shortly.'

'Is that right?' he said.

'He hasn't anything to do with this,' cried Lauren.

'Indeed he has. When one of our well-known inhabitants ends up facing a knife, then it is our business, mam'selle. That he saved you is praiseworthy, but we need to get to the bottom of this. The man's description will be circulated and we shall take our inquiries from there.'

'When shall I have my passport back?' she asked.

'In a few days. Don't worry. I hope you both have a very pleasant evening.'

'I'll show you out,' said Jean-Luc.

When he came back, Lauren was sitting down.

'They think I'm a criminal!'

'No!' he replied. 'This is the police. I told you what they're like. Provincials.'

'I'm sure they did. I don't what Gary is going to say. He'll probably go crazy.'

'You're the injured party.'

'It didn't feel like it. Perhaps I should get in touch with the British Consul?' She was thinking about her passport.

'We can talk about it if you want—and I can pull a few strings. Please, let's forget it for a few hours. I have been most remiss in not asking you if you are hungry. If so, we can go and have dinner immediately.'

At that moment, Lauren felt as if she couldn't eat a thing. What was happening? Who would want to kidnap her? What was this to do with Gary or his contact, Belleville? The whole thing made her feel sick.

'The table is booked at the Coq d'Or,' he added. 'I eat there a lot. It will be a special menu.'

'Thank you, Jean-Luc, but I should go back.'

'Please, let me do this,' he said. 'I confess that our first meeting was less than auspicious.'

She frowned and he added, 'The auto route stop?'

'Oh.' She smiled in spite of how she was feeling.

'Even then, in that brief moment, I felt I wanted to know you better. I wondered if I'd ever see you again, which I know is ridiculous, but here you are. Do you not think it strange that we should meet again in such peculiar circumstances?'

'Maybe it was Fate,' she confessed.

'Fate has never been kind to me. Let us call

it a happy coincidence instead.'

Yet a mean little voice sounded in his head suggesting that coincidences like this were few and far between. Could she really be trusted? He was a wealthy man and as for Belleville and her boss having a meeting . . . But he squashed the doubts. He believed otherwise. For instance, how could she have known he'd be in the garden at that moment? It was ludicrous.

'Ok, I'll come.' said Lauren, 'But then I'll have to go back and sort this out.'

Inwardly, she was thinking about Gary's meeting with Belleville. And Belleville was in business with Jean-Luc. What did it mean? *What's the matter with you?* she asked herself. *He saved you from Heaven knows what?*

Lauren had always expected this holiday of Gary's wouldn't be easy, but she hadn't expected this. However, if she hadn't agreed to accompany him to the South of France, she wouldn't have met Jean-Luc, and she wouldn't have wanted to miss that.

'Sorry, I have to go to the bathroom and, the answer to your question is yes.' He raised his eyebrows. 'I'm absolutely famished. I haven't had a decent meal all day.'

'Good,' he said. They smiled at each other.

*   *   *

The Coq d'Or had become part of the dream now.

'It's lovely,' she said looking through the window down at the harbour. She'd seen lots of wonderful places on her travels the last couple of years, but this evening and this view were different . . . Jean-Luc was by her side.

Below, the bay smouldered under the dull red of a fast-disappearing sun and the rippling waves had become lines of encroaching fire.

She stared at the menu, spoiled for choice. They had chatted over an aperitif and the day's problems had paled again and she found herself laughing spontaneously. Jean-Luc was fun. How could she have thought him sad? He was thrilling. He had a way of making very moment count.

'Ready to order?' he asked.

'So much on offer,' she said. 'I think I need some advice.'

'What about my favourite?

'Which is?'

'A secret.'

'I can't risk it.'

'Alright . . . appetisers. Avocado mousse, followed by langoustines, then bombe cassis.'

'Goodness,' she said.

'You said you were hungry.'

'I am. I'll go for it.'

He waved and the maître d' trotted across.

'Pierre. My favourite—for two.'

Lauren was looking round. The furniture was authentic antique and the high-back carved chairs had clawed feet finished with golden claws. She imagined Paul's comments. He was Left in his views, but he didn't say no to the perks Gary's money brought. The few patrons of the restaurant appeared to be the same ilk as Jean-Luc—wealthy and probably well-known.

She looked up at the cockerel painted on the wall, its head ringed with stars, standing on a coat of arms and realised it was the same that she'd seen on the side of his Ferrari.

'That crest is on your car, isn't it?'

'Yes.' He leaned forward and whispered, 'I own this place.'

'You're going to tell me you own all that next.' She was looking down at the harbour where the stars danced and twinkled in the advancing dark.

'A substantial part.'

She stared at him. She'd been joking.

'Some boutiques, a beach or two, a handful of villas and a couple of yachts at the last count.'

'Stop!' she said, 'You're scaring me. You'll tell me in a moment Gary hired the villa from you.'

'He may have,' he said. 'I shall have to ask my agent.' His lovely face broke into a grin. 'Only joking.'

The idea worried her. It would implicate him in whatever was going on. She changed the subject.

'You know, that first time I saw you I had

the impression you weren't happy.'

He looked at her. 'You were right,' he replied.

'You should be. You—' she gestured. 'You have all this, but . . .' The waiter was beside them.

'This is Michel,' said Jean-Luc.

'Mam'selle.' He gave a tiny bow then commenced to open the wine Jean-Luc had ordered. He handed a glass for Jean-Luc to taste. Jean-Luc continued when Michel had gone.

'I am not happy—nor unhappy. Perhaps I am bored.'

It was a half-lie. He was with Simone, but he had his father's affairs to attend to. At present, he relished neither. The police visit had disturbed him. They had investigated his father's sudden death and so far the answer had been an open verdict. He asked himself then, *What am I doing? I should be finding out about Belleville rather than sitting here entertaining a beautiful woman.* But, at that moment, he desired nothing more in the world.

'So you're a jaded aristocrat?'

'Who plays rugby.' He grinned.

So you keep thinking about what happened too, thought Lauren. 'I'm glad it was your sport. That was quite a tackle!' she added, returning his wry smile.

The meal's superb presentation was

equalled by its taste. It arrived in small portions in the French manner. Carrot hearts and mange touts arranged artfully in a small basket. The avocado mousse followed by the langoustines, which she tackled bravely, taking her cue from Jean-Luc and heaping the shells beside her plate and washing her fingers in a silver bowl. In fact she was noticing everything about him. Especially that he only drank one glass of wine. Finally, the rich red dessert delicately floating in a carmine sea was placed before her.

'It's fantastic,' she exclaimed as she tasted it. She leaned back. 'Thank you, Jean-Luc for a wonderful meal—and a wonderful evening.'

'I hope it isn't over yet,' he replied and meant it. 'I would like to hear something about you, Lauren,' he said. 'For instance, how you speak such good French.'

'Thank you,' she said, 'but there's not much to tell. I'm very ordinary.' She was thinking what different lives they led. If she was sacked from her job or resigned, she probably wouldn't be doing this very often. Unless . . . she didn't know if there could be an 'unless'— but she wanted there to be.

'But here goes,' She began sketching out her background. 'My grandmother was French.'

He looked pleased. 'Lauren, I see—but not James.'

'Lauren, perhaps, but my grandma married an Englishman, a soldier. My own parents weren't well off, but my dad was in the Services too and travelled around a lot. So they sent me to boarding school, a convent, run by an Order of French nuns.'

'A convent! That's not so common any more.'

'I suppose not, but I liked it—sometimes. I suppose that's why I like France. Boarding gets you used to being away from home and I'm good at languages. Probably one of the reasons I pulled off the job with Gary. I have my uses.'

Jean-Luc was smiling now. It seemed to Lauren that in the candlelight he was more handsome than ever, his whole face dominated by his dark, expressive eyes and mobile mouth. His chin was strong and his nose was perfect. Every girl's dream. *And I'm part of it*, she thought.

When he spoke, she was fascinated by the expressive way he used his hands and she could have listened to him all night. She could very easily fall in love with him, she concluded and it made her feel shaky.

He was looking at her intently, then he leaned back.

'Your turn!' she said.

So many things he couldn't tell her. He was a private person and found it difficult to trust anyone. He had been looking for some girl to understand him, someone he felt at peace with. When he looked at Lauren, he felt a strange warmth inside he couldn't remember feeling for any girl. There had been so many who were interested in his fortune. He'd found them in the casinos, on the catwalks of Europe, starlets on yachts and most were like Simone. He had always admired beauty and elegance, but he had found it cold and now, facing him was a vibrant, young woman who seemed interested in him for himself.

Maybe he was being naïve, but he was enjoying the feeling. He didn't mention his personal sadness that his mother became reclusive after his father died when she'd handed over all her affairs to Belleville, who had been her father's long-time friend and whom Jean-Luc didn't trust. Unfortunately, it was an unspoken assumption that Jean-Luc and Simone would tie the knot and all their fortunes from their fathers' diamond dealings would be secured. However it wasn't working out that way and the diamond dealings were now an anxiety.

As for Simone, she had been always a brat and now, she was an equally spoiled young woman. She treated Jean-Luc and the Villa des Anges as if it were her property already and he had been foolish enough to go along with it.

The only person he had ever discussed such things with was his aunt, Catherine, who lived in Monaco. She was the only person he could trust now. Yet he'd travelled far and enjoyed the privileges of the rich, so he told Lauren about his house in Martinique and his yacht and some copious traveller's tales.

They talked and talked. Michel, who had waited on Monsieur Hilarie's special guests many times decided his patron looked very happy and his lover was beautiful. Michel knew all about lovers, because he'd had much experience of them as they wined and dined in secret. He would say that these two were happier than most. He had never seen Monsieur behave like that with the blonde girl.

Certainement, he said to himself as Jean-Luc signalled him, *Monsieur is a very lucky man.*

*   *   *

The maître d' held the door of the restaurant open and they walked through into a strong wind blowing up from the sea.

'I can get a cab, you know,' Lauren said, even though it was the last thing she wanted.

'No cabs,' he replied. 'I promised to take you home. Eros is waiting. Come.' He slipped his hand into hers and it felt both exciting and comforting all at once. She was thinking what she'd say if he invited her to stay over—she knew what she'd like to do—as they walked on up the road.

She shuddered a little as they passed the doorway into which she'd been dragged a few hours ago. He must have sensed it as his grip tightened.

93

They were outside the gates now. Trying to take her mind off what had happened, she asked, 'Why did you call your car Eros, Jean-Luc?'

The name was so cheesy! She knew already, she just wanted to hear him tell her. Eros was the god of love and sexual desire. Yet, everything Lauren heard from him tonight had changed her original opinion of him as a playboy and certainly not a guy who might see his car as a badge advertising his sexual prowess.

He was using the code on the gate instead of the control. She thought he might be offended by the question.

Once inside, he paused. 'Do you really want to know?' he asked, an amused expression on his face.

'Sorry, I was only being facetious,' she apologised.

'I understand your motive for asking,' he replied.

They were very close as they walked on. She could see the dark shape of the Ferrari huddled in the drive. He took out his keys and its lights flicked on and a minute later he was holding open the passenger door. She did her best to slide into the low-slung sports very conscious of how much leg she was showing.

'I'll tell you in a minute,' he said, his eyes on her legs. He went round, settled himself into the driving seat and leaned back. The lights in the car went out. He put out his hand and took hers. They were a breath apart.

'Eros, he said. 'My first Eros was a Testarossa, the choice of a very hot-headed youngster, who thought it suited his image which was that Eros responds to women and is very fast.'

Jean-Luc looked so whimsical and contrite that she laughed.

'Since then every one of my cars has remained Eros, and yes, if you are asking if I have changed . . .' he paused, 'I have grown wiser, but the hot-headed boy has not quite disappeared.'

He let go her hand and next moment was pulling her close.

The kiss that followed was passionate yet tender and she responded to his embrace, which seemed to last ages in its aching loveliness. She closed her eyes, savouring the strength and sweetness of his mouth. Finally, he let go.

'The Jean-Luc of the past would not be sitting here now. He would . . .' his voice was tantalising, 'He would be offering the girl a bed for the night, but this one . . .' he put his hand over his heart in the most enchanting Gallic gesture, 'He has the feeling it wouldn't be the right thing to do—although he would like to very much . . . Lauren?'

She breathed in. It was up to her—and she didn't want to spoil the magic—or to make a mistake like she had with Gary. The thought of him brought her to her senses.

'I think I like the Jean-Luc as he is now,' she said.

'I thought that. Spoken like a convent girl.' He made a face. 'There is plenty of time—that is, if you still like me.'

'Yes,' she said.

He reached over, kissed her cheek and pulled the seat belt over her breasts. She knew what he was thinking.

'I really have to go, Jean-Luc because . . .' She didn't want him to think she was some kind of prude—or that she didn't want him. 'I know I should explain. It's because of . . .'

'Mr Grey.'

'Yes.'

She was happy he didn't ask her why. He was looking at the digital display.

'But our night is not over yet, I still have something to show you.' He pressed the ignition and the engine roared. Laurel noted the 330k on the speedo.

'How fast does Eros go?' she asked. Gary wouldn't let her touch the Land Cruiser. What would it be like to drive a Ferrari?

'220 English mph. But don't worry. I shan't be doing that tonight, although that hot-headed young man comes to life on the auto route.' He grinned like a little boy.

They left the environs of Grimaud and turned on to the main road. The Ferrari's acceleration was exhilarating and its cornering superb in the hands of its master. Lauren's head was swimming with car and stars. Jean-Luc had that rare quality—allowing a girl to feel completely safe, yet causing her to be strung-up with nervous excitement.

'Where are we headed?' she asked as he negotiated a sharp bend. The ton of car held the road securely.

'My favourite place.'

Neither of them spoke for a while. Lauren was looking up at the moonlit sky as the beautiful landscape flashed by, white villas, tall palms and, on her side, the ink-dark sea with its slicks of white reflecting the gorgeous moon.

Eros nosed its way off the road down a narrow deserted lane, which finally opened into a grassy area on a high cliff face looking out to sea. The engine throbbed, then ceased. They were alone in the space and silence. His tanned hands still held on to the wheel as he and Lauren stared out to sea.

'I've always loved this place,' he said. 'And the sea. Did I mention that the Hilaries were pirates once?'

She smiled. 'No, and you don't look in the least like a pirate.' She found himself imagining him as a half-naked Sinbad. He reached over and took something from behind the seat. A magical package covered in tiny, silver stars. He was holding it out. She frowned,

'What is it?'

'Open it and you'll see.'

'But whose is it?'

'It's for you. As a thank you for tonight.'

'I should be thanking you,' she said.

'I want you to have it. Besides, you didn't get your roses.'

'What roses?'

'I have a confession to make. After I saw you in the street this afternoon, I had this feeling I wanted to find you.'

'You mean you recognised me from the auto stop?'

'You knew me, too. I could tell.'

'Yes, but . . .' she didn't know how to answer.

'So I took a walk into town to see if I could bump into you by accident and I bought this— and a bouquet. Just in case. I'm afraid I gave it to Cecile in the end. Do you mind?'

She was staring at him—he'd been chasing her! He even looked apologetic about it. She had a wild feeling of elation as she looked down at the package.

'Of course not, but I don't expect anything in return for a magical evening,' Lauren said, staring at the package 'I couldn't accept anything,' she added.

'Not even the roses, if I still had them? Wouldn't you have taken them if we'd met?'

'Well . . .' Lauren was at a loss for words.

'I'm French,' he said and shrugged. It was such a marvellous little gesture.

'The roses perhaps, but a present . . .' She shook her head.

'Please open it, even though you don't want it.'

But she did want it, very much.

'If it was pirate booty, would you take it?' He looked mischievous as her fingers fumbled with the ribbon.

'No,' she replied, smiling.

He sighed as the box was revealed. It was mother-of-pearl and shaped like an oyster, glistening in the moonlight. Her fingers trembled on the catch and he put his hand out to help her. She felt a sharp stab of pleasure at his touch.

The oyster's shell sprang open to reveal the most exquisite rope of pearls Lauren had ever seen and she gasped at their milky-whiteness, which glowed against the blue velvet background.

'Jean-Luc,' she breathed. 'How could you think I'd take these. They must be worth a fortune. They're exquisite, wonderful, marvellous but . . .'

'But?'

'It wouldn't be right. We've only met. You don't know me.'

'I know what you've told me,' he said. 'I want you to have them. You've made me very happy. I can't remember when I enjoyed myself so much. Besides, they'll suit you.'

He could see by her face he'd made a mistake, but it had been worth it. He told himself he had to be careful now in case he lost her.

'There's no way I could accept them,' she said. It was too much. It was like a dream—sitting in a Ferrari with a handsome man and being offered exquisite jewellery. 'You must see that, Jean-Luc. I can't possibly accept these from you.'

'I can see I've made a mistake,' he said. 'It was just to say how much I've enjoyed your company.'

Lauren waited. Maybe he was going to tell her that he didn't want to see her any more. If he did, then she would know this wasn't anything special.

'These mean absolutely nothing,' he continued, 'and believe me, I want to see you again, but now I'm scared.'

She hadn't been expecting that. Scared?

'Scared that you're offended now and maybe you don't want to see me again?'

'I do very much, but . . .' she whispered. 'But it's just like a dream. It's too much.'

'I understand,' he said, turning and pressing the ignition. 'I was wrong. I don't know how to . . .'

He shrugged his shoulders. He was going to say, 'I don't know how to treat women,' because the women he'd been out with would

100

have taken them and probably laughed about it with their girlfriends. Simone would have thought nothing about them.

'Please, Lauren, try to forget the pearls.' She saw him take in a deep breath, then he turned and added, 'It might have been worse. It could have been diamonds!'

She closed her eyes, shook her head and they both laughed.

'Is that your business?' she asked. 'Diamonds?'

'Unfortunately.'

She swallowed. 'Gosh,' she said.

'Yes. Hilarie & Belleville, Diamond Importers and Exporters, Monaco. Is that Mr Grey's business?'

'Not that I know of,' she said. 'He told me he was here to research his latest travel book.'

'Then he must have other things to discuss with my partner.'

'I suppose so,' she agreed, but as she looked through the window, she was thinking about Gary's mysterious trip to West Africa, which was supposed to be about a book as well. That seemed dead in the water too!

As Jean-Luc concentrated on the road, he decided that he was going to start checking if Grey's firm had any business with Maurice. If it had, he didn't know anything about it. If it was anything illegal, it would be another lever to rid himself of Belleville and also it might throw some light on what had happened to

Lauren that afternoon.

*   *   *

'I've had a marvellous evening,' Lauren said as Jean-Luc brought the Ferrari to a halt the other side of the small bridge in the Square.

'So have I,' he replied, his eyes lingering on hers, her lashes, her cheeks, her mouth, the rise of her breasts . . .

He turned and undid her seat belt, then he took her in his arms and kissed her again on the mouth. Flames leapt inside her and she wanted to feel the whole of his body beside hers, to stay with him for what was left of the night.

But they broke apart and Jean-Luc glanced at his watch. The solid gold hand pointed to near dawn.

'You have a key?' he said.

She nodded. 'When I can find it!' She looked up at him. 'They didn't want my bag, Jean-Luc, so what did they want? I shall be looking behind me all the time from now.'

'That might be a good idea,' said Jean-Luc, 'But I'm sure the police will get them soon.'

'Here it is.' She produced the key.

'Which one?' He was looking at the houses as they walked over the bridge.

'That one—over there.'

He looked. It was one belonging to a subsidiary they used.

102

'It's yours, isn't It?' Lauren stopped. 'I don't know how to say this, but could this all be coincidence?'

'I don't know,' replied Jean-Luc frowning, 'Believe me, Lauren, I know nothing about Grey's business.'

She was going to say, *You should, you're the boss,* but she didn't. Probably everything was delegated in his world.

She was strung-up by his kiss and was waiting for him to ask her out again. He'd said he wanted to see her again, didn't he?

'I can't ask you in. You do understand?'

'Yes. We'll be in touch, very soon.' He produced his phone. 'Your number?'

She was so relieved. Then she put the key in the lock and grimaced. He waited until she managed to open it.

'Will you be alright?' he whispered.

'He's only my boss,' she whispered back.

'If you're not sure, I could come in.'

'No, if he were up, it could make things worse. I can handle him, but he's probably out.'

'Ok.' He looked uncertain. 'Well, good night, Lauren. I've enjoyed every minute.'

He kissed her on both cheeks—twice—then a moment later, he was walking over the bridge towards Eros.

What a first date that's been, thought Lauren happily as she slipped inside, then peeked back out. He was still sitting in the car, but that moment he started the engine.

How could she think Gary wouldn't hear the roar—unless he was drunk, of course. She walked quietly towards her bedroom door, but a moment later, she felt a tap on her shoulder.

'Good was he?' Gary asked. The look in his eyes scared her.

'Yes, and I'm going to bed now.' He caught her arm, hurting her. 'Leave me alone!'

'You've some explaining to do first.'

She felt almost too weary to remonstrate. It was like someone had put the light out in her and she couldn't be doing with all this.

Wriggling out of his grasp, she faced him. His monogrammed dressing gown was wide open revealing his bare chest and that he was only wearing his pants. The immaculate waves of his hair were rumpled and his face was dull and angry. His eyes looked as if he hadn't slept. She could smell drink on his breath.

'What the hell have you been up to, Lauren? What time do you call this anyway? You've been to bed with him, haven't you?' He grabbed her again.

'Let me go!' She twisted from his grasp. 'What if I have? I'm fed up with this attitude of yours. I only work for you, Gary. And you'll have my resignation in the morning.'

He put out his hand and twisted her body against his. She knew with horror that she was too tired to put up a fight. As she struggled to get away, a voice said.

'Leave it, Gary, you're drunk.'

'Paul!'

She ran to him and he motioned her towards her bedroom.

'Watch it,' he said to Gary and unlike the Paul she knew, his voice was hard-edged. 'Leave her alone or I'll be handing in my notice too and then where will you be? You need me.'

Gary stopped as Lauren rushed through her bedroom door and locked it.

She lay on the bed, staring at the door for ages, hoping Gary wouldn't come after her, like he did last night, but there was silence. It wasn't until then that she thought about what Paul had said. Whatever he had, it had done the trick, but what hold could Paul possibly have over Gary? What did he mean that Gary couldn't do without him. That he needed him?

She closed her eyes. All an exhausted Lauren knew was that she was going to find out as soon as she could, but how? She'd just given in her notice.

CHAPTER FIVE

Lauren didn't sleep well, especially as she hadn't come in until about 5am. She felt washed-out, but nothing, not even her decision to quit, could quench that excited feeling of meeting Jean-Luc again.

However, she ached all over and her discovery in the shower that she had bruises in all kinds of places brought yesterday's attack into focus. Coupled with handing over her passport, it made her feel vulnerable, which wasn't a good place to be, considering her problem with her job and Gary.

Lauren told herself she'd done the right thing last night. He couldn't behave like that to her any more. She shook her head as she showered.

Could she keep yesterday quiet? She knew she needed to find out why anyone would want to kidnap her. It hadn't even been dark. Perhaps whoever was in that car believed she was connected with someone they were after, some unknown quantity. Yet it was the tie-up that really disturbed her. The man who'd attacked her would have seen her come out of Jean-Luc's villa. Maybe they thought she was something to do with him?

She was now. Jean-Luc was connected with a man she'd never met—Belleville—and so was Gary, which made her an innocent accessory.

Lauren realised then she was afraid they might try it again. They hadn't tried to steal her bag, her passport or her phone. They only wanted her which was even more terrifying because she knew nothing.

You won't find anything out now you've quit,

106

she said to herself, as she dressed and tamed her wet curls. Lauren felt scared, puzzled and angry. She didn't want to be in this position, whatever it might be. As for Jean-Luc, she couldn't believed he would be involved in something shady.

Then she shook her head, he was very wealthy. Jean-Luc's business was diamonds. That was no joke.

As for Gary, he definitely might be into something dodgy. *You don't do things by halves, Lauren,* she thought. You need to know what's going on and if you quit you won't.

*   *   *

Paul and Gary were sitting opposite each other when she entered the living room. Paul looked at her intensely.

'No full English this morning, but I've a feeling that you wouldn't want one, like someone else.'

She nodded. Gary didn't look up.

'I'll make myself scarce then.' Paul picked up his camera. 'If you want me I'll be taking some shots of the boats. See you.' *So you're ducking out,* she wanted to say, but kept quiet. Paul's look had said *It's between Gary and you now.*

She sat down and reached out for the coffee pot.

'Good morning,' she said. It was all in the

open now. Gary's eyes were still red, otherwise he looked as slick as usual.

'I'm sorry,' he said. 'I don't know what came over me.'

She sighed. After all, it wasn't the first time.

'I don't want it to end like this.'

'You remembered then,' she said.

'You're giving in your notice.'

She picked up her coffee and took a sip. 'Yes.'

'Can I persuade you to stay?'

'I very much doubt it. I'll work out the month.'

'Please, Lauren,' he put out his hand. 'It . . . it just drove me mad to know that you were with him.'

'I realise that, but that's what it's going to be like from now on,' she said. 'I like you, Gary when you're reasonable, but you're a pig when you're drunk. The fact is, I don't love you and I've had plenty of time to find that out. You said I was in the minority and I probably am, but that's me. If you can't understand that you'll have to find someone to replace me.'

'I don't want anyone else,' he said, putting out his hand. She ignored it.

'I thought you were going to rape me last night!' she suddenly burst out.

'I'd never do that!' he retorted, shocked.

'What about the night before? What were you going to do then? I can't work with someone who behaves like this.'

'I know,' he said, 'But I am sorry and it won't happen again. You have my word. Will you give me another chance?'

Lauren looked at him. He seemed to mean it. It would suit her to stay, but not under these conditions.

'Let's leave it open,' she said. 'Any more and that's it. And I'll have you for sexual harassment.'

She wondered then if she'd gone too far. He didn't answer, but took a deep breath and poured himself a cup of coffee.

'There's no hope for us?'

She couldn't believe he wouldn't give up.

'Did you hear anything I said?' She stood up.

'Don't go off on one, please! I promise I'll behave,' he replied. 'Shake on it?'

'I don't think so. At the moment I'd rather you kept your distance physically. It's strictly business from now on.'

She sat down again and broke a chocolate croissant in half.

'Right.' He withdrew his hand. They looked at each other, then Lauren carried on with her breakfast.

*   *   *

At the Villa des Anges, Jean-Luc wasn't enjoying the beautiful Mediterranean morning or the sun that was flooding in through the open French windows. Outside the terrace paving was a carpet of curled rose petals driven into heaps by the Mistral.

He had a huge amount of paperwork but he kept on staring at the phone. Was Lauren up yet? He couldn't wait to speak to her. He knew just to hear her voice would make him feel better after the confrontation he'd had with Simone half an hour ago.

He hoped she'd be gone by now. He'd expected her to be jealous, but this time she'd gone too far. She'd appeared at his breakfast table and even had the nerve to come back to the villa and sleep in her bedroom last night! Nothing put off Simone. He guessed she'd checked to see if he'd slept with Lauren.

They'd had a massive row. He told her it was all over and had asked for her key back. She still thought it was a joke. He breathed in deeply. He'd almost lost his temper with her. He'd never struck a woman but he'd been near to doing it. Even then she brazened it out. She was like a limpet who was stuck to him. She was a selfish, scheming bitch.

He felt worried, not for himself which would be ridiculous, but for Lauren. Simone might do something to her, but what could she do? The only way to stop her was to humiliate her publicly. Jean-Luc wasn't a fan of humiliation, but perhaps, when Simone saw he was serious about Lauren and he wasn't on the market any more, he might get rid of her once and for all.

He picked up the phone on his desk.

Simone stood on the terrace by the open French windows, but out of sight. When she peeked and saw him on the phone, she guessed it was to the girl. Simone had come into the garden late last night, and let herself into the Villa des Anges. Jean-Luc wasn't home, which made her mad. She would have gone back and spent the night with François on the yacht, but he'd already taken *L'Hirondelle* to Monaco for her birthday party. The real reason for Simone's visit was to find out if Jean-Luc was sleeping with the English girl, but his bed was empty. He didn't come home until after five; she heard the Ferrari and concluded he must have taken the girl somewhere—a hotel perhaps.

Jean-Luc was Simone's property and the girl was going to pay for it. She was planning that at the moment. She understood Jean-Luc very well and knew he had strong feelings about truth and loyalty. He also hated publicity. That's why he and she weren't getting on at the moment. He suspected she and François were having an affair, but so far he hadn't openly accused her, because people would talk. That's how it had happened the last time she found someone else for a while, but he'd always taken her back. She'd find to way to get round him again. He was never going to find the woman of his dreams—she'd see to that— and certainly it wasn't going slumming with

111

some pathetic publicity girl. He was looking for class.

When she'd met Gary Grey yesterday and took him over to Jean-Luc's, she could see the Englishman was besotted with his PA and he was jealous. Simone knew all about jealousy! She'd been cheating on Jean-Luc for a while, but had to admit although she liked François' body, he didn't have the cash to maintain her lifestyle. Now she had a rival which she didn't like.

She'd come down for breakfast with a smile on her face.

'Good morning, darling,' she said, planting a kiss on Jean-Luc's cheek.

He looked up at her. 'What are you doing here? How did you get in?'

'You gave me a key, remember,' she replied. Jean-Luc was more interesting when he was angry.

'I'll have it back then.' He held out his hand and she stared at him and smiled.

'That isn't a very nice thing to say. It's my birthday party tonight. Or had you forgotten?' He shook his head. 'You know what I want.'

'Simone, we've talked about this before . . .'

'Yes, I know we're going through a bad patch—why, I can't imagine—but we'll be all right again.'

'No, Simone, we won't. We're finished.'

'Jean-Luc,' she said, shaking her head. 'We're not. We always get back together.

We're made for each other.'

'We're not,' he repeated.

Simone loved winding him up. 'We know each other too well to split up—and last time we did, you came back. Admit it, you couldn't do without me.'

'But now I can.'

Simone felt very angry as she faced him. 'Just keep deluding yourself with this new woman, Jean-Luc. I can tell you it won't work out. She's nothing.'

His face was hard. 'I've had enough, Simone.'

'She's a gold digger. Just look at her. At least, I have my own money.' She giggled.

'Oh do be quiet!'

'Touched a nerve have I, sweetie? That's all she wants. You'll find out I'm right and come running back to me.'

'I've been running after you too long.' His eyes flashed.

'Wow,' she said, 'You're exciting me. She'll turn out to be a jewel thief or something. By the way, you have jam on your face.' She put out a finger and touched his cheek. 'Just there.'

He pushed her hand away. 'What do you mean?'

'Diamonds, darling. All girls love diamonds. You said you'd bought my present.'

He looked at her. 'You are unbelievable! Didn't you take any notice of what I just said?'

'How many times have you asked me that? It's part of my charm. And that's what you like about me.'

She sidled up to him again and he pushed her away hard, she fell back against the chair, then he charged off to the office.

That push had settled it. It was the girl's fault. Things usually didn't get that far. He was too laid back for violence. Her eyes narrowed. Lauren James was going to pay for this. She pressed herself against the wall and listened to the conversation.

*   *   *

Gary was still sitting at the table, looking through the window. Just as Lauren was deciding what to do next, her mobile rang. 'Excuse me, I have to take this.'

'It's him, I suppose.' Gary jumped up and walked off, but she knew he was listening, so she went into her bedroom.

'Jean-Luc,' she said, 'It's so nice to hear from you . . . Yes, I'm alright, I'm having my breakfast . . . Yes, everything was fine. Thank you for last night.'

They talked only briefly as she explained Gary was around. 'Are you at home?' she asked.

'Yes, up here at the villa. However, I want to ask you if . . .' he paused. 'If you would to come with me to Monaco.'

'When?'

'Today. I can pick you up.'

'I don't know.' She wanted to, desperately. A party on his yacht sounded marvellous, but she'd have to get back to him.

'I can't say for sure . . . you know why,' she said before she said goodbye and shut her phone.

A party in Monaco. That wasn't going to make Gary very happy! But she was going to ask nevertheless. She went back to the kitchen and he was at the table again.

'That was Jean-Luc. He wants to take me to Monaco today.'

He swung round. 'Actually, I'm going there today myself. I was going to take you anyway. And Paul. It's just that I had other plans for us.' She raised her eyebrows. 'Ok, I promised. I won't say anything. I'm seeing Belleville again at some do he's giving. A party. I was hoping you'd come.'

'Maybe I would—if Paul is. But I shall still meet Jean-Luc.' She could see Gary was trying to control himself.

'I thought hc was an arrogant prat when I met him.'

'You weren't too nice yourself,' she replied.

'Well, as you said it's your life. You'll have to leave it until the afternoon. I can't spare you before,' he said.

'Fair enough, I'm sure he'll go along with it. What do you want me to do this morning?'

'Check a few people out.'

'Sure. I'll go and get my lap top.'

When she reached the bedroom, she sat down on the bed and rang Jean-Luc back.

'He said yes . . . I know! Of course everything's ok . . . but he wants some work done. I'm afraid I can't make it until the afternoon—and I'll have to travel with him . . . Sure . . . Wait a minute I'll take the address down.'

She went to fetch some paper and a pen.

'By the way, he's going to a party. It isn't . . .?' She stopped and listened to Jean-Luc.

'No! You don't mean we're all going to the same party? Yes. It's at Belleville's . . . Simone's birthday . . . Oh, I couldn't! . . . Yes, I know I'll be with you, but . . . Come on, you don't mean that surely . . . I don't know what to say . . . Yes, I've packed something. Is short ok?'

They chatted on for a few more minutes before she shut the phone, her whole being a riot of excited apprehension. She couldn't imagine what was going to happen. He'd invited her to Simone Belleville's birthday party! Simone and Gary there at the same time. It sounded a nightmare, but she couldn't say no, because inside she had a warm glow of satisfaction. Gary and Simone would be so gutted! It would serve them right.

Lauren just hoped what she'd brought with her would be suitable. She had the choice of four dresses, two smart cocktail and two long formal. At that moment, she was pleased she worked for Gary. Although she couldn't afford Dior, what he paid her was enough for a decent designer. She couldn't go wrong with black—or white?

She'd have to change somewhere, too as she couldn't possibly meet Jean-Luc in the day wearing one of the two. He said he was going to take her to meet someone for tea first. Maybe she could change there? That bit was very exciting, but the rest of the evening she couldn't envisage. And as to what to do about yesterday . . .

Finally, she decided not to tell Gary that she had an invitation to the party from Jean-Luc— unless he asked her. The invitation had also opened up an opportunity. Maybe she could find out something about Gary's business with Belleville?

Her next problem was whether or not to tell Gary about the assault and that the police had confiscated her passport.

*   *   *

Later in the morning when they were almost ready to leave for Monaco, Gary took a phone call. When he put it down, he was in a foul mood.

'Aren't we going now, boss?' asked Paul. He glanced at Lauren.

'Oh, we're going alright,' he said. 'I wouldn't miss the trip for the world.'

'Great,' said Paul. 'Are you looking forward to it, Lauren?'

'Can't wait,' she said.

'I bet you can't,' replied Gary.

His worst suspicions had been confirmed. Simone Belleville had found Lauren and the Frenchman in bed. She was really upset on the phone. She'd asked him for help. Hilarie had been two timing the poor girl, especially as she said that he and Simone had been planning on getting engaged at the party.

*   *   *

Jean-Luc left in the Ferrari after lunch. He was still angry after the exchange with Simone, who'd gone off in a huff.

'See you in Monaco,' she said spitefully. 'I assume you'll have come back to your senses by then. And I once thought you were a gentleman!'

He didn't trust himself to answer when she flounced off.

Then she stopped and called, 'And don't be late. I want my present.' She had the nerve to grin.

'I'll be there,' he called, 'Considering it's my yacht.'

Yet he was feeling almost ashamed at what he was about to do. He knew he might be putting Lauren in a difficult position, but he was going to tell her what he planned, then she'd have the option. He also needed to go to *L'Hirondelle* before and see that another place was laid for his guest. Simone was in charge of the arrangements. He was fed up with the whole thing. He and Simone weren't kids any more playing games. He'd always let her win to keep her quiet, but this time she wasn't going to. Let her do what she intended to do. He didn't care what she'd say about him, because it wasn't true—and he would explain to Lauren. At that moment, he wanted to see her more than anyone else in the world.

He didn't even notice the scenery on the drive, nor the car following him. Monaco was somewhere he'd done things he hadn't been proud of, but as he'd told Lauren the night before that was his other self. Once thing he was sure of, he'd been a good friend to a lot of people and his business reputation was good— or at least he thought it was.

Which brought him to Belleville.

As he drove towards the harbour he'd made the decision. The party was exclusive and he was fairly sure that he could get Belleville on his own. Maurice had a few things to explain. Jean-Luc was also very curious as to what role Mr Grey had to play in his recent business.

Jean-Luc parked Eros, then walked through the lines of yachts until he reached *L'Hirondelle.* She was large, but dwarfed by a couple of Russian-owned yachts at the end of the line.

But there's not one like her, he said to himself with an owner's pride. He'd had so many offers to sell, including one from Maurice when his father died. Maurice was the last man whom he'd sell to anyway. Jean-Luc always had dreams he'd sail off somewhere in the world which was much simpler, a place where he could be himself—and with someone he cared for.

He had been looking for that girl for a long time—and now, he wanted to believe he'd found her. Simone knew how to get to him. Lauren wasn't a gold digger and he intended to prove it.

When he stepped on to the yacht, no crew were around, not even François. Jean-Luc swore. He could understand the crew being on leave as Simone had hired staff for the evening, but his yacht master—where the hell was he? He walked around. Not on the bridge. He went down the stairs and listened at the door of François' quarters. Silence. It was slightly ajar so he pushed it open and entered.

The room was empty, and the connecting bedroom door was only half closed. Sleeping on the job, he thought and looked in.

François was asleep, one leg hanging over the bed, his arm thrown over the girl's naked back. Jean-Luc went cold. Simone! He could see they'd been drinking and he felt sick with revulsion. He backed out quietly and sitting at the yacht master's desk, took the wrapped box containing the diamond pendant out of his bag. Grabbing a piece of paper and a pen he wrote.

Your birthday present. For services rendered. Tell François when he wakes up that he's sacked. Set another place at the table, I'm bringing a guest.

Jean-Luc.

Then he got up, went back to the bed and put it on the side table by Simone's head. With one last grim look, he left.

He was trying to calm himself when he walked onto the jetty. He didn't care about her making a fool of him again—but with his yacht master! That was going too far.

You knew it was going on though, a little voice said in his head, *you've known for ages.* He breathed in deeply. He needed fresh air— away from the smell of the two of them.

He thought of Lauren and looked at his watch. It seemed for ever until he met her. He allowed himself to smile. Whatever Simone had insinuated, Lauren was not like her. He believed she would never betray him like that.

Picking up his other packages from the Ferrari, he made his way to The Hermitage. He'd have time to arrange things before he met Lauren in the hotel foyer. Then he'd explain what was going on. He wasn't going to have to worry about doing the dirty on Simone

121

any more.

The men who were waiting in the shadows let him pass, then they made a sign to a car, which started up and followed the Ferrari at a distance. It was high-powered enough to chase it if it had to. The men withdrew into the shadows, remaining to watch the yacht.

*   *   *

Half an hour later, Simone and François were sitting naked on the bed. François was looking at the note then he tore it in half.

'We're screwed now. What the hell are we going to do?' he asked. He put his hand on her breast and she pushed it aside.

'What do you suggest?' she said. 'He knew anyway.'

'What are you getting at?'

She laughed at the question. 'It's quite clear,' she said. 'You're fired.'

He stared at her, an incredulous look on his face. 'You mean I'm dumped?' He swung his legs over the side of the bed.

She watched, amused. 'Let's face it, darling, he's only sacked you. He might have hired a couple of hit men.'

'But I thought you loved me?'

'What? Oh, you poor darling.' She drew her hand down his back and he quivered. 'You've got a lot he hasn't, but well, no money!' She shrugged.

He put his head in his hands.

'Well, that's it,' she said. 'I'd get packed if I were you. The kitchen staff and the waiters will be here soon. You wouldn't want to be still here when he comes back. Such a pity you're so poor though.'

She walked round the bed and stood in front of him. He looked up at her naked body.

'What if I weren't?'

She frowned. 'What do you mean?'

'What if I had as much money as him.' She collapsed, laughing. 'I'm not joking,' he said.

'Where is this money? Is that why you're a yacht master and you don't own one? Why I pay your bills?'

'I have money. More than him—or at least as much as him.'

He was staring at her. Simone sat down beside him. 'You?' she said, 'Where is it? In the bank? Stowed away in gold bars?'

'I won it,' he said. 'At the Casino.'

'You are priceless.' But she was beginning to look interested. 'Where is it then? Where are the bank statements?'

'Before I show you anything, you have to promise.'

'I don't do promises,' she replied, 'before I have evidence.'

'You're everything to me.' He grabbed her.

'Hey, you're hurting me.' She rubbed her slim arm. 'Look, you've made a mark.' He kissed it hard but she pulled it away. 'So where's this money then?

'If I show you, will you come away with me? Today!'

'Don't be ridiculous. It's my party. But, if it was worth my while, I could come tomorrow.'

François lit a cigarette and walked round the room. He was more controlled now. 'I'll show you.'

'You're crazy,' she said. 'I don't believe a word of this.'

'You will when you see it. It's right here. On the yacht, but if you're thinking of telling the police, you're dead.'

'Ok,' she said warily, 'Why would I tell anyone? I suppose—if it was worth my while I might come along with you for a ride.'

'Hilarie doesn't want you any more, Simone, he's dumped you. You've no yacht, no boyfriend . . . but I want you.' Simone's eyes narrowed. 'What would you have left? An old dad, who dotes on you, but who's as bent—' He stopped.

'What about my father?'

'You didn't know, did you? Your old man's up to a lot of shady things. Sooner or later, they'll catch up with him and you'll be left with nothing.'

'How do you know this?' Her indignant eyes flashed. 'It can't be true.'

'I can prove it is,' he said. 'I know.'

'How?'

'I can't tell you—yet. Your father deals in

diamonds, dirty diamonds, Simone, with a lot of dodgy people. They're not a very nice bunch. I can give you a good life. I'll make you love me. You'll have everything you want.'

'Who are these people?'

'Better you don't know,' he said.

'Make me believe you about the money then,' she hissed.

He nodded. 'After I've shown you, I'll go to the bank and withdraw the rest. We'll need some ready cash. We'll meet at a train station. Not an airport. I'll text you.'

'Station? I haven't been on a train for ages,' she said.

'I'm not joking, Simone. And if you breathe a word to anyone, I'll kill you. And if you're not serious,' he said, going over to a drawer, 'Then I'll have to kill you because I've told you.'

'What's in there?' she asked, her eyes glinting. 'Is that it?' She came over and stepped back. 'For God's sake, François, that's a gun!'

'If you want to get your own back on Jean-Luc this is the way, Simone. You and I take off with the money. He'll pay for what he's done to you in ways you can't imagine.'

'It's not your money, is it? You didn't win it at the tables?' Her voice shook a little and he ignored the question.

'We'll take the train out of Monte Carlo, find an airport—and then who knows—Rio, the Caribbean? Anywhere you want.'

Simone was looking at the gun. She sat down.

'Put on your wrap,' he said. 'I'm going to show you now. Then you can make up your mind. But remember what I said.' He took the gun out of the drawer and put it within his reach while he pulled on his pants and jacket.

'And if I don't come with you?'

'Then I'll come back for you. One day when you're not expecting me. And it won't be nice.'

Simone was really scared. She put on her wrap.

'And from now on, you keep your mouth shut.'

She nodded.

*   *   *

An hour later, the two men waited outside the bank. Earlier, one of them had walked in and looked around. He could see François at the grille and the bank teller was counting out the cash. It had taken some time to sort out such a large transaction near to closing time. François waited, trying to look nonchalant. He had no idea he was under surveillance.

The man emerged and made a brief call on his mobile, then closed his phone and nodded to the other. It was the go ahead.

When the yacht master came out with the holdall, he looked round as if he was scared someone would see him.

The two shadows followed him in the direction of the yacht harbour, then separated at the point agreed. Snatching him in daylight was risky, but the duo were used to working together. He took the short cut as they'd expected and turned into a less busy thoroughfare lined with parked cars.

As he turned to cross the road, his way was blocked and then he could feel a gun in his ribs.

'Shut up and do as I say.'

François nodded, terrified. The other man joined them, took the holdall containing the cash and François was forced to walk across the road and up another street where a car was waiting. As soon as he was inside, a hood was pulled over his head and his hands secured.

As they drove off, he was begging, 'I don't want to die. If you let me go, you can have the money!'

Twenty minutes later, after an agonising drive, François was pushed, stumbling, into the entrance of a large villa. He was still begging for mercy as the door slammed behind him.

CHAPTER SIX

Lauren parted from Gary and Paul in front of the Casino. 'Here's where I'll be staying tonight,' said Gary, handing her a card. His voice was as cold as it had been all the way to Monaco. 'I've booked you a room there. Whether you'll be needing it or not . . .? he shrugged.

'Thanks,' she said, ignoring the inference.

'And I'm leaving around ten tomorrow. Don't do anything I wouldn't, wherever you're going.' He looked at her, 'And don't go spending all your money or you'll be asking for a rise.'

Lauren grimaced as she collected her things and started to get out of the back. Naturally, she'd been relegated from her favourite seat. Paul jumped out of the front and opened her door.

'Green-eyed monster,' he whispered as he took her things and put them on the pavement. 'He'll get over it. You know my number if you need me.'

'Thanks,' she said looking round.

'Cabs are over there.'

'Great. Thanks again, Paul.'

'Be sure he looks after you. Where you going—just in case?'

'The Hermitage. For tea.'

'Wow—Monsieur Hilarie knows how to treat a girl. Now I'm jealous, too,' He grinned. 'You won't actually need a cab there, but I suppose you can't turn up there carrying your luggage.'

'What are you two mumbling about?' shouted Gary.

'I'm sorry for you, Paul,' said Lauren.

'I know how to handle him,' he replied. 'Have a good time.'

He bent and kissed her on the cheek and she was taken aback. She watched them screech off, then crossing the road made her way to the cab rank.

*   *   *

The cab dropped her right outside the front entrance. She looked up and the hotel was breathtaking and very close to the sea. Where else would a girl have a date with a millionaire, thought Lauren. It was exciting, but if she'd been looking only for money, she'd have taken up with Gary.

She caught a glimpse of herself in a window and decided she looked good. She was wearing a simple but expensively-tailored white shift dress from Jaeger with a matching short jacket and pretty sandals. She had no option but to carry her evening wear in the bag it had come in, which was Dior label. The black dress had finally been her choice and she was counting

129

on being able to give it a quick press as it was pure silk. If she'd bccn staying here, she'd be able to send it to be pressed, but she'd only been offered tea. She'd also brought a wrap which had been in the Liberty sale, which complemented the dress perfectly.

Lauren climbed the steps and as she entered she was dwarfed by the foyer's magnificence. The predominant colour was deep gold with the ceiling supported by great yellow marble pillars. She didn't have to go to one of the reception desks, which resembled podiums rather than the normal check in, as with great relief, she saw Jean-Luc hurrying forward to meet her.

She took a deep breath. He looked marvellous and she was seeing him wearing a suit for the first time, which showed off his athletic figure more than the sports jacket. The suit was silver grey and quite obviously bespoke.

'Lauren,' he said, kissing her on both cheeks, then lightly on the lips. 'You're here.'

'Did you think I wouldn't make it?' she quipped. 'This place is marvellous,' she whispered, looking round. 'I much prefer it to modern décor.'

'I like it too,' he answered, smiling and looking round with fresh eyes. He'd been used to the place for so long he hadn't really noticed. 'Come on.' He took her arm. 'By the way, you look lovely.'

'Thank you.' She'd been in many fabulous hotels with Gary, but never one like this with a man she . . . her inner voice was suggesting 'loved', but she tried to ignore it. It was too soon, but she did like him very much—and falling in love with might be even better.

Now he was by her side, the hotel's opulence was exciting rather than overpowering 'And we're taking tea here?'

He smiled down at her. 'I hope you don't mind, but we're sharing it with a relative.'

She stared at him.

'Don't worry.' he said, 'I only have one.' He wondered then if he'd gone too far, too soon. Yet he wanted to show her off. 'Tante Catherine, my only aunt—she has lived here for a number of years. She gave up her home voluntarily. I tried to persuade her not to, but she wouldn't hear of it. She wanted to be in town, for the shopping!' he shrugged in a whimsical manner. 'I can see you think it strange.'

'No, no, I'll be delighted to meet her—but I'm a little . . .' She searched for a word. She was scared but she wouldn't say so.

'A little apprehensive? Don't worry, she's been forewarned.'

Lauren couldn't help laughing at his expression. 'I'm pleased.' She patted his arm. 'But don't you worry either!'

'I'm not. She'll be enchanted by you.'

Yet Lauren was quaking inwardly as

they passed into the lobby where they were acknowledged by two smiling doormen, who knew Jean-Luc by name. He ushered Lauren towards the lifts. One door slid open to reveal a uniformed operator and soon they were moving up the building.

'Tante Catherine has a suite here. It took her a long time to make up her mind which one she wanted, because she said she couldn't do without a sea view.'

Then he bent and took the opportunity to kiss Lauren hard enough to make her pulse go mad. The operator seemed to be completely oblivious.

'I had to,' he said.

'I don't mind,' she said. 'In fact, if the lift wasn't stopping I'd ask you to do it again.'

The lift stopped and the operator didn't open the door until Jean-Luc let her go, then the doors slid open. As they walked out, he nodded to the man, who acknowledged them with the hint of a smile

'I hope you don't do that kind of thing all the time,' she joked as the doors closed.

'From now on, I'll do it every time,' he said. 'If you like it.'

Lauren was breathless. He guided her along a corridor. 'Nearly here,' he said.

They paused in front of a white door. 'Just a moment,' Lauren said anxiously. 'What shall I call her?'

'Tante Catherine,' he replied.

'You're sure she won't be offended?'

'No, she's very easy to get on with.'

Lauren hoped so. She'd been imagining a wealthy and ancient doyenne whose wishes were granted on the run, but she couldn't have been more wrong. Tante Catherine was as charming as her nephew.

She appeared to be in her early sixties and elegantly-dressed in a short-sleeved powder-blue trouser suit, silk blouse and pearls. She had the same smile as Jean-Luc and Lauren warmed to her from the very beginning of their conversation, and she could see that Tante Catehrine and Jean-Luc were very close.

The suite itself was bigger than a small house with fabulous antique furniture and all kinds of precious artefacts and family pictures which Tante Catherine explained, pointing out where she had obtained this or who was that past relative. Lauren was fascinated. They took tea on the white terrace overlooking the harbour. Jean-Luc leaned over Lauren's shoulder and pointed.

'You see that yacht on the first row?' She nodded. 'That's mine. *L'Hirondelle*. It's where we're going tonight.'

Catherine turned to Jean-Luc. 'That girl,' Lauren knew she meant Simone, 'Should have had her birthday party in a hotel. Really, Jean-Luc, when will you learn?' She turned to Lauren and asked, 'Have you met her, Lauren?'

133

'Yes.' Lauren hadn't known it was Simone's birthday party!

'Ah, I have a feeling that you and I have the same opinion of her?' She regarded Lauren with bright, questioning eyes.

'Enough about Simone, Catherine,' Jean-Luc said, getting Lauren out of an awkward position.

'It's looks like a marvellous boat,' Lauren said, changing the subject. 'I've been on a 30-footer, but never on one that big.'

The Hilaries regarded each other and Tante Catherine smiled.

'Jean-Luc likes the best and in my opinion the past is just that,' Catherine said.

'You see, Lauren, *L'Hirondelle* is not new; she belonged to my father.' Lauren caught the sad look in his eyes again.

'His yacht is not like those awful Russian ones, dear. They're stupendous, but vulgar.' Catherine made a gesture of distaste. 'Come, now, more tea?'

'Thank you,' Lauren nibbled at a tiny heart-shaped pastry, which tasted like a real strawberry.

'Mmmm, heavenly,' she said. 'Oh,' she remembered, 'This sounds rather strange, but owing to Jean-Luc's unexpected invitation and seeing that I'm travelling light, would it be possible for me to press my dress?' She felt a little foolish.

'Wonderful!' said Catherine and there was

134

nothing patronising in her tone. 'Call the maid, Jean-Luc. I don't iron these days. I did once, in the past, but that's another story.'

'Well if you two are going to talk about ironing, I'm going to pour myself a drink and make some phone calls,' Jean-Luc said. 'I'm sorry, but I need to check a few things.'

'Go ahead, Jean-Luc, Lauren and I can manage quite well without you.'

'Back soon,' he said, smiling at Lauren and picking up a tiny cup cake, he put the whole of it in his mouth at once, then he walked across and opened the adjoining door to Catherine's study, which Lauren had seen on the tour of the suite.

'Children, my dear,' said Tante Catherine, shaking her head. Lauren looked at her, startled. 'All men are children. Best to let them get on with it.' Lauren sighed in relief, but it was shortlived. 'Now I'd like to hear something about you.'

Their conversation wasn't tricky after all. Lauren explained about her home and upbringing and she discovered that Tante Catherine's father had been in the Services too.

'Free French, dear.' She'd been educated in a convent too. 'That explains your accent,' she said, 'I'd like to compliment you upon your French,' Catherine said, 'I don't want to be insulting, but the English are usually hesitant to display their abilities in a foreign language.'

What Lauren wanted was to find out more about Jean-Luc and she was eventually rewarded.

'The boy was devoted to his father. I'm sorry to say his mother died early. She was a lovely girl and he takes after her.

I tried to help the two of them, but no-one can take a mother's place. Consequently, he has made some difficult choices—particularly with his girlfriends. They tend to be beautiful but most unsuitable.' She frowned.

'In what way, Tante Catherine?'

'Like Simone Belleville. The girl has been after him since she was a child, selfish and spoiled, but he's come to his senses.'

'But . . .' began Lauren, 'We hardly know each other. We only met yesterday.' Of course, that wasn't strictly true and she didn't add anything about their second meeting.

'Oh, he won't declare himself for a time, but he's on the way. I can see it in his eyes. He's not the hot-head he used to be, but I can tell he likes you, Lauren—a lot—but he's not very trusting these days after all his disappointments'

I wonder how many he's had? thought Lauren.

Tante Catherine continued, 'I hope that things are going to develop between you. I like you, Lauren, and I shall tell him so. Now excuse me. I'll go and see how your dress is getting on.'

Lauren exhaled with relief as Tante Catherine headed off in the direction of the kitchen. While she was gone, Lauren got up and stared at the yacht again. What she could see of it was so beautiful, but Simone was holding her party on it. That just didn't make sense. If he was finished with her for good, why didn't he tell her? After all, it would probably ruin her birthday when he turned up with someone else on his arm.

Too fast, Lauren, she said to herself. You don't know what's really going on between them. They've known each other for ages, even though they're behaving as they can't stand each other. Take it easy, although he must really like me to introduce me to Catherine. For approval.

She grimaced and wondered how many other girls he'd taken to see Tante Catherine. That was a little bit worrying—and then she thought of him and her heart started to race.

Catherine hurried back. 'The dress is hanging in the guest bedroom.' She checked the ornate clock on the mantelpiece. 'Six already. Perhaps you should change now?'

'Are you sure?'

'Of course. And may I say I think you've made a good choice with that dress, dear.'

'Thank you,' replied Lauren, warming to her even more.

'Let me take you through,' said Tante Catherine. 'I think that Jean-Luc is going to show you the casino. It's very interesting.'

Lauren nodded in response. She supposed that when the Hilaries gambled—if they did—they dressed for the occasion.

As she shut the door behind Catherine, Jean-Luc emerged.

'I've sent her off to change for the Casino,' Catherine said. 'Wise choice. Best you've made. Now sit down and tell me all about what's going on with Belleville's daughter and how you're going to get out of that mess!'

*   *   *

As Lauren dressed, she was thinking about the shock Gary was going to have when he realised she had been invited to the party too. She had mixed feelings about it; maybe he'd freak out. Then she told herself he had more sense than that. It would look bad for business. As for Simone, she might go mad too and she was more dangerous than Gary, in a subtle way.

Lauren realised she was going to have to be very careful. She trusted Jean-Luc, but he had put her in a difficult position, which didn't make sense. If he'd been a different person, she might have thought she was being used. She expected most of the girls he'd been out with would have revelled in getting their own back—and she admitted to herself that in a way she was already feeling the thrill of turning up with him and having her revenge.

However, she needed him to tell her why this was happening. As far as she knew he wasn't aware Gary was going, but he'd probably guessed. That was the way big business was done; invitations to private parties.

She ought to tell him she'd heard that Gary had an appointment with Belleville on a yacht. Maybe Belleville had a yacht himself and it wasn't the same party, but she doubted it. Perhaps it was a trial, like meeting Tante Catherine to see how she coped. She hoped not—and she hoped that he was going to tell her some time soon.

She stared at herself in the long mirror. The sleeveless dress was the most expensive one in her wardrobe and she'd brought a bag which was right in fashion, a portfolio clutch of a reasonable size, She smiled. It was so much better than a tiny one. She felt she looked right.

She heard a knock on the door. 'Come in.'

Jean-Luc's eyes were full of admiration. Lauren has not expecting him to be wearing a tuxedo. He looked divine! Hc put his hand inside his jacket and produced the oyster-shaped box.

'Oh, no,' she said, 'I couldn't!'

'Please,' he said. 'Wear them for me—just for tonight, if you like. They'll suit your dress perfectly.'

She gasped as he brought them out. He

fastened the diamond clasp and she stared at herself in the mirror.

'I knew they would suit,' he said and he kissed her.

A few moments later they emerged.

Tante Catherine looked them over and remarked. 'You make a wonderful couple.'

Lauren knew she was looking at the pearls, but she was well-bred enough not to remark upon them. All she said was, 'I'm glad some young people still dress up to play the tables. No place is the same as it used to be, such awful people around these days. So many East European billionaires.'

Jean-Luc smiled at Lauren.

'I know you're laughing, Jean-Luc, but that is my opinion. Nothing is the same as it was. It was all so marvellous when I was a girl, Lauren.'

'I'm sure it was,' Lauren said.

'We have our own casino here in the hotel and it suits me to lose my money there. My dear, I hope you have a wonderful time and make sure he looks after you, or you come back to me and let me know. And don't wish that girl a Happy Birthday.' Her eyes twinkled as they said their goodbyes.

A moment later, they were walking down the corridor.

'She's amazing,' Lauren said as they waited for the lift.

'I know. And you are too. It's going to

happen again.'

'I hope you will take me to see her again,' she said misunderstanding.

'I mean this is,' he said, taking her in his arms. 'I've been wanting to do it for the last two hours.'

Then she was in his arms and they were sharing a kiss that lasted so long and was so passionate that Lauren felt dizzy when they broke apart. She hadn't heard the lift arrive, which was waiting, its operator observing the same correct etiquette of staring at the buttons as if oblivious to the whole thing.

'Ground, sir?' he asked as they entered.

Jean-Luc nodded. As they reached their destination, Jean-Luc put his hand in his breast pocket and produced a currency note.

'Thank you, Charles. I'm afraid it's a habit we're finding difficult to break!'

'Yes, sir. Thank you, sir.'

Charles grinned and pocketed the tip, then the lift doors slid shut behind them.

Jean-Luc took her arm. 'We've some time before we're due at the party, so how about the Casino?'

'That would be great,' Lauren said, feeling a thrill at the thought of making an entrance with as handsome a man as Jean-Luc to accompany her.

*　　　*　　　*

As Gary flicked back his hair, he was feeling vicious at the thought of what Lauren might be doing now. What he felt for her was something he hadn't experienced before, but she had made it clear she wasn't interested, which presented him with a dilemma: could he work beside her and not keep his hands off her? He'd been hoping this trip would make their relationship stronger. He told himself he'd taken a big risk doing what he was now— and it was all for her. He knew that she liked the good things in life and he'd spent a lot of money on her already and he'd intended to give her a raise as well.

The more he thought about Lauren the more disgruntled and angry he became. He'd find some way of paying her back. How dare she give her notice in and go off with some playboy!

Maybe he ought to ditch her when she came back from the Frenchman's bed like she had last night and she'd had the effrontery to resign. He could have slapped her but he concluded it wouldn't have been worth the hassle and anyway, he could get himself plenty of girls.

'You've done it this time, Lauren,' he said out loud. 'You'll be sorry you ditched me.' The whole thing made him sick.

'It's the first sign, boss.'

'What?' Gary glared at Paul.

'Talking to yourself.'

Gary merely snarled back.

'Time for the party,' replied Paul.

If he didn't need him so much, Gary might have punched the photographer right in the face, but the fact was Paul was a vital part of the deal with Belleville.

'Come on.' Paul said. 'I shouldn't sack her if I were you. It'd be much easier for all of us if you kept Lauren on side. She knows nothing and that looks good for you, ok?'

Gary charged out of the room with Paul following.

'Keys?' Paul held out his hand. 'I'll take them to reception. You go straight out to the car park. I need to buy some ciggies.'

Gary nodded, handing the key card over. 'Make it quick,' he said, 'I don't want to keep the old man waiting.'

Still seething, Gary walked through the lobby and out of the revolving doors, where he stood on the steps. Why the hell hadn't Paul just asked one of the staff to bring the car round?

'Damn it!' he said, the night wind ruffling his hair. He brushed it back with his hand and made his way round the back to the car park, taking the car keys out of his pocket.

A moment, later, he was about to the flick the open switch, when someone grabbed him from behind. He could feel something hard pressed into his back.

'Just come quietly, Mr Grey.' The voice was

English.

'What the bloody hell's happening?' he shouted, trying to turn round.

'That's a gun in your back,' said the other man, who was now walking beside him.

'What's going on? What are you doing? Who are you?'

'You'll find out soon enough,' the man said.

Gary began to struggle, but his arms were pinned to his back and he was quickly overpowered. He looked round and saw that Paul was behind him. He was smoking a cigarette and made no move to help.

Gary went crazy. 'You double-crossed me, you bastard! Help, help! Someone! Help!'

Gary suddenly found himself staring down the barrel of a gun.

'That was stupid,' the man said. He had an expression that was devoid of any emotion. A large car had driven up beside them and he said, 'Come along, Mr Grey. Quietly.'

He nodded to Paul, who walked off.

Seconds later, Gary was pushed into the back, where a man was already seated.

'Good evening, Mr Grey,' he said, then nodded to the driver, who accelerated.

'What the hell are you up to?' Gary said.

The man turned to him and said in a patient but disturbingly cold voice, 'We hadn't planned to kill you right now, but if you don't shut up, we just might.'

Gary closed his eyes. All he could think of

was that he'd been betrayed. As the car slid away and negotiated the corner of the building they passed Paul, who nodded at them, threw down his cigarette and walked back in the direction of the hotel.

*   *   *

There was some delay getting into the Casino. Jean-Luc had indicated Lauren should sit down while he went off and spoke to an official. A few minutes later, her eyes were dazzled as they walked through into the atrium of the grand hall.

The floor was paved in marble and there was a profusion of great onyx pillars. The place was massive, devoted to every kind of gambling. They walked over to a secluded area, which was guarded by an official, who nodded to Jean-Luc. They walked up some steps and inside the room, where people were laying their bets on a roulette table. It was very James Bondish.

'What was all that about outside, Jean-Luc?' Lauren asked. 'It was something to do with me, wasn't it?'

'Yes. I would have normally taken my guest into one of the private salons in the Grand Casino, which are for the high-rollers,' he said. 'We're not that tonight, darling, otherwise we'd never get to the party. This is a half-way house.'

145

'But we were stopped?'

'Yes, because we need to show a passport. It would be even worse if I lived here because Monegasque aren't allowed in at all. Luckily, I don't. I'm not keen on Monte Carlo, I'm a country boy at heart.' He laughed.

'We shouldn't have come, That must have been really embarrassing for you.'

'Not at all. They know me well. I told them you'd forgotten to put it in your bag. Don't worry, we'll get your passport back soon. Let's forget it now, Lauren. I'll thought you might like to have a small gamble.'

'I've never played before.'

'Not even with your boss?'

'Gary? No, he's too tight!'

'How boring,' said Jean-Luc. 'Then you should try. I'll show you how.' Someone was already behind them, pulling out her chair and she felt as if she was in a Bond movie.

'I think I'd rather watch you,' she said.

'We'll make up this table. They need about eight.'

She looked round at the other occupants. Luckily, none of them appeared to be the sort who had a revolver hidden their purses! They were all formally dressed and she realised entry might be denied into this room without the right clothes.

Lauren started to wonder if he was a gambler and, as if reading her thoughts, Jean-Luc turned to her once he was seated and said,

'I find gambling fun, but those days are over, but I thought you'd like a little flutter. We can leave if you wish?'

'No of course, it's very exciting.'

She watched two men who seated themselves opposite. They certainly looked the part—close-cropped hair, bullish—and she avoided their glances. Jean-Luc spoke in rapid French to the croupier and a pile of coloured chips were pushed towards them. She stared at them, thinking they were going to be playing with a lot of cash.

'I don't know what to do next.'

'Choose a number from the wheel,' he said. 'If we win, then we exchange these for cash chips.'

Lauren had seen it on the movies, but now it was for real. She'd always been up for a challenge, but this? Her mind went blank for a moment. The croupier was waiting for the bets to be placed. She glanced across at the piles of chips in front of the opposite players.

Jean-Luc said, 'Go on, choose and I'll make the wager.'

'Twenty-two,' she said impulsively.

'Red or black?'

'Red.'

She was trembling as Jean-Luc pushed all the chips forward. 'Vingt-deux, rouge. Your birthday?' he said.

'How did you know?'

'Most people do that, but they rarely choose

mine.'

'The twenty-second of what?' she whispered.

He put his hand over hers. 'I'm a Leo,' he said as the croupier started the spin and launched the ball.

'No more bets. Now watch—you might be lucky.'

She watched, fascinated and her heart beat accelerated as she felt his arm slip round her and, as the wheel spun, he gave her a kiss on the cheek. It seemed as if the whole room were spinning around her as if she was going to wake up soon. She watched as the ball fell into the slot. She couldn't believe it!

'You've won!' he said. 'Would you like to put it all on again?'

'I couldn't,' she said.

Jean-Luc was looking at his watch. 'So let's call it a day, then.' He nodded, got up and stood behind her to pull her chair out for her. Then he picked up the chips. 'Next stop the cash desk. I knew you'd enjoy it,' he said. 'Tante Catherine does.'

'I won, I can't believe it,' she repeated. She looked across and saw that some of the other gamblers were smiling, except the sinister pair. As they walked away, she whispered, 'They know I haven't played before.'

'They just like looking at you,' Jean-Luc whispered back, 'and they envy me—and you; some of them will be losing a fortune tonight.'

'Do you come here much?' she asked.

'Only with business clients these days, but I thought you might like the experience. As the English say, first time lucky—and you've made a packet!'

He made her laugh often—and she loved that.

'It's your money,' she said.

'No, you chose. I have no luck on the tables and have learned my lesson, so I don't play any more,' he said. 'But I liked watching you enjoy yourself. How about a special cocktail?'

The bar was as Lauren imagined, understated elegance, with gold-beige leather chairs to sink into. She could see the glorious terrace outside, overlooking the harbour.

The barman hurried over. 'Cocktails, sir?'

Lauren couldn't choose. There was such variety. 'I don't know what to have,' she said.

'Do you like rum?' Jean-Luc asked. 'And peaches and oranges?' She nodded. 'Then I'd recommend this one,' he said. 'Bacardi, peach Schnapps, fresh mint leaves, fresh orange, Rock Candy syrup and Sprite.' He looked up at the waiter and added, 'Two, please.'

'Yes, Monsieur Hilarie.'

When it arrived Lauren sipped tentatively from the tall glass. It was wonderful. 'Wow,' she said.

He laughed, then looked at his watch again. 'It's nearly party time.' She had to ask him about Simone now, seeing he didn't seem to be relishing the prospect.

'Jean-Luc, can I ask . . . I know it's on your yacht, but why are we going to Simone's party? She's in love with you and I'm going to spoil her birthday.' He looked very serious and she waited a moment, but then added, 'I have to ask.'

'You're wrong, Lauren. Simone's in love with my money—and my name. I'm finishing with her for good tonight.'

'And . . .' she hesitated, '. . . and are you using me to do it?' She had to know. 'If you are, you should know I'm not happy about it.'

He put his hand out and took hers. 'I was going to explain,' he said. 'I found her in bed this morning with François, my yacht master.' Lauren gasped. 'I sacked him and she knows it's over. I also told her I was bringing a guest and she'll know I mean you. She's cheated on me before and . . . well yes, I can see it in your eyes, Lauren,'

'What?'

'You think I'm a coward. That I took her back because I'm in love with her, but I never was.' His words were forceful. 'At first, in the beginning I suppose we had something, but was a long time ago. I've known her forever and she was always spoiled, but I've been a coward, I suppose. I went out with other girls, too. She didn't like it, but I didn't either like her behaviour either. I told you I'd grown up and come to my senses. I didn't want that kind of arrangement even then.

'I never met anyone I loved. If I had, I'd have been faithful. I'm not like Simone. She's only jealous of you because she knows this is the real thing.'

Lauren stared at him. He'd said it was the real thing!

'You've only just met me, Jean-Luc. I don't want to be a pawn in any game you're playing.'

'Please, Lauren, I want you with me tonight because with you, I feel whole again, that I've some purpose in life.'

Lauren was amazed. 'I . . . I really like you . . .' she said, 'But I wasn't expecting this.' She was remembering what Catherine had said—*he takes a long time to declare himself.* Here he was professing that he couldn't do without her.

'I know, but I feel inside that we're going to be together whatever happens. You've saved me, Lauren.'

'No, you saved me, but are you that sure I'm the right girl for you? Things like this just don't happen. I've been to all kind of places since I've been working for Gary, but I'm just ordinary—and you're not; you're wealthy, you have a different lifestyle. You like me, I know, but . . .'

'No, Lauren, I'm falling in love with you. Don't you feel it?'

She lowered her eyes and replied softly, 'I do, Jean-Luc . . . but I'm afraid . . .'

'Don't be. Whatever Catherine said about

me in the past, I'm different now. Please believe me, Lauren—and don't turn me down tonight.' It was the last thing that she wanted in the world. 'Please give me a chance.'

She took a long, deep breath. 'I will,' she said, 'And I might as well come clean too. I'm pretty sure Gary is going to be there. He told me he was going to a private party on a yacht. You asked me last night whether I was alright with him. I'm not. I handed in my notice because his behaviour was intolerable.'

'What did he do?' Jean-Luc's voice had lost its gentleness.

'He was horrible, but Paul intervened. I've made it clear that if it happens again, I'll walk out. He's jealous, Jean-Luc, because I haven't . . .' She couldn't bring herself to say *slept with him.*

'He'll probably be feeling exactly like Simone when he sees me with you.' Lauren smiled in spite of herself. 'So, I'm really doing the same as you are. I'm sorry that I seemed to doubt you,' she said, 'Because they both deserve it.'

'Thank you, Lauren,' Jean-Luc replied, looking at her with desire showing plainly in his eyes. 'After we've collected this, we'll head off and get it over with.' He took out the cash chips.

When he turned round from the cashier's window he said, 'Here.' He was holding a wad of notes. 'It's yours.'

'No, it's your money,' Lauren protested.

'I didn't win it. Take it. There's seventeen-and-a-half thousand Euros,' he whispered. 'I wish I'd put on a thousand now.'

'What?' Lauren gasped. 'That's over thirteen thousand pounds!'

'Thirty-five to one,' he said. 'The odds on a single number win. Great feeling, isn't it?'

'I can't take it, really,' she said.

'Here.' He took her bag. 'Put it away and straight in the bank tomorrow. You can use my safe on the yacht if you like.'

'We'll talk about it later,' she said. She was feeling dizzy as she placed the roll of notes inside and clutched it to her tightly.

'Anyone would think you'd robbed a bank, Lauren,' he laughed. 'Would you like to walk instead of take a cab?' he said. 'It's not that far.'

'Yes, please, I need some air,' she said—and she meant it.

The night was getting more like a dream every minute. She'd just won a fortune on the tables—well, it seemed like a fortune to her. Lauren didn't notice the two men watching them. She only had eyes for Jean-Luc. As she and Jean-Luc walked off, one was making a call on his mobile.

CHAPTER SEVEN

The sky over the harbour was streaked with pink and red as they walked towards the yachts.

Lauren looked up. 'It's all so beautiful.' she said. Jean-Luc didn't speak, only kissed her, then draped the wrap about her shoulders before they walked on arm in arm. Inside, Lauren was rehearsing what she was going to say when she went aboard.

'Don't worry,' he said. 'I'll be here, right by your side.' She knew then that she never wanted him to be anywhere else. He squeezed her arm. 'She can't hurt you. Neither can Gary.'

'I know,' Lauren was all strung-up and not only because of his nearness. She was already imagining the sensation their entrance would cause. 'Oh, I forgot,' she said, 'Who else will be at this party?'

'Mainly Simone's friends and her father, Maurice Belleville.'

'What about your friends?' He only shrugged and she added, 'I'm sure you have some.'

'Yes, but surprisingly, they aren't party goers.'

'You'll have to tell me more,' she said. 'I don't suppose Simone's father will be very happy.'

'Shall I let you into a secret? I hope he isn't. I don't like him any more than you do.'

'He's your business partner and you don't get on with him?' She didn't really want to pry but she wanted to know more.

'Let's say it's a long-standing disagreement,' he explained.

'Yes, I know about those,' she said, managing a smile.

As they reached the gangway he said, 'Chin up, as the English say. We'll face it together. We're late, so I'm afraid we'll be making the grand entrance.'

Lauren's heart was beating fast in her ears. As they reached the yacht, a security man approached.

'Invitation, sir?' he said.

Jean-Luc smiled. 'I am Monsieur Hilarie, the owner. And this is my guest.'

'Yes, sir,' the man stood back.

Jean-Luc didn't move. 'You're being paid to ask for our identity,' he said and withdrew his papers. The security guard looking shamefaced, checked Jean-Luc's card and waved them on. A moment later, Jean-Luc was helping Lauren on to the deck, where she could hear vibrant music.

The yacht was festooned with lights, which would have been magical if she'd had the time to appreciate them, rather than think of meeting Simone.

'It so beautiful,' she said, looking round, 'And so big.'

'Not that big. About 115,' he replied, 'But she's fast.' His face lit up with enthusiasm, like it had been when he told her about Eros. 'Boys' toys, I'm afraid.'

Yes, a Ferrari and a fast yacht, she thought.

'My father bought her in the States in 1988. I wouldn't let her go for anything. She's great for partying. You can get over sixty people in the salon.'

'Will there be that many?' It sounded like a nightmare.

'No, she's probably invited about thirty. Hold on tight.' Lauren didn't need an invitation. 'They won't all be staying over. In fact, there'll be only two left on board tonight.'

The remark couldn't have been more pointed. 'You'll like the state room,' he said. 'Actually there are four of them. All mod cons. I had them re-furbished last year.'

Lauren would have been infected by his enthusiasm, if she hadn't been worried about Simone's reaction.

They were met by a smiling waiter offering champagne, followed by another carrying an array of canapés. Lauren shook her head at the champagne, but chose a canapé of choux pastry, which when she nibbled was filled with some kind of soft herb cheese and ham. Jean-Luc followed suit. When they walked in, Lauren looked round, estimating that there

156

were at least twenty people.

Just as Lauren noticed the ornate cake, Simone emerged from a knot of people. Her face was expressionless as she came over to them and embraced Lauren. It was the most uncomfortable moment so far as Simone hissed in her ear, 'You think you've won, don't you, but you're wrong!'

She let go and beamed, 'Jean-Luc, darling.'

Instead of embracing her, he slipped his hand into Lauren's.

'Is everyone here? François, for instance?' His face was set into a mask. Lauren had never seen him like that before. 'Good,' he said, 'I think I should go and introduce Lauren to some of guests.'

Simone wasn't to be so easily put off.

'Thank you for my beautiful present, darling.' She purred and stretched up, planting a light kiss on his lips. He stood silent. Simone let go, turned and hissed at Lauren, 'You'll pay for this,' and flounced across the room to join a small group of people who were murmuring amongst themselves.

Lauren was trying to hold it together. What kind present had he given Simone— and why had he, when he was going to dump her? For the first time, she found herself almost doubting Jean-Luc's intentions, but those disappeared as he looked down at her, squeezed her hand and gave her a reassuring smile. 'Well done,' he said.

157

She was conscious of several people watching them, one in particular, a short grey-haired man, impeccably dressed, who approached them. He was looking Lauren up and down and his expression was a mixture of hostility and lechery.

'You've brought a new friend with you, I see, Jean-Luc.'

'Yes. This is Maurice Belleville. Maurice, my girlfriend, Lauren James. She's English.'

'Delighted,' he said, making the word sound like a threat.

Lauren could feel the sudden hush, then the chatter began again. People were looking at her and whispering.

Jean-Luc drew her aside. 'I think they're getting the message, don't you?' he said. 'Keep strong, you're doing well. I'm proud of you.' She looked across the room to where Simone was standing with a gaggle of fashionable women, loaded with diamonds. Everyone was glowering.

Jean-Luc whispered in her ear, 'Courage. Don't be scared of them—although I am!'

'I'm not,' she said and smiled.

'Good. Remember, I'm proud of you.'

He returned to his conversation with Simone's father, while Lauren stood as near to him as she could. She breathed in. As yet, there was no sign of Gary. It wasn't like him to be late. Maybe it wasn't this party he was going to after all.

Simone was on her way over for the second round. She was wearing the most stunning multi-coloured silk sheath dress which probably cost thousands.

'What have you done with Mr Grey, Miss James? Have you dumped him?' she asked.

'He isn't mine to dump,' she replied, keeping her cool. 'Did your father invite him?'

'I did,' she replied, 'While you were out, stealing other women's fiancés.'

'Fiancé?' Lauren hadn't expected that.

'Yes, I'm getting engaged to Jean-Luc tonight. He's a terrible philanderer, but I can handle him. He does these things in fun. It's a game we play. Don't you feel a teeny bit anxious?'

'Not in the least,' replied Lauren, realising that people were straining to hear. 'Besides I think it is up to Jean-Luc whom he gets engaged to. And I don't believe you anyway.'

'You little tart!' Simone's insult was delivered in an icy whisper. She was so up front with her insults that Lauren was almost beginning to enjoy it.

'You're not wearing the ring then?'

Simone's expression was less than pretty. 'No, it's in here,' she said, 'He gave it me today.'

'I would have thought you'd want to show it off. He told me you're very fond of diamonds,' replied Lauren.

If the whole thing hadn't been so awful she

would have laughed at Simone's expression. The girl must have thought she could be intimidated. If Lauren could put up with Gary's mood and behaviour, she was definitely Simone's match. After all, she couldn't throw her out.

'Why don't we go and finish this talk in the Ladies' room?' said Simone. She looked murderous.

Well, if you want a cat fight, you might get one, thought Lauren. Her patience had run out.

Jean-Luc turned and touched her arm. 'Are you ok, Lauren?'

'I'm fine,' she said, 'Simone is just going to show me her engagement ring.'

He looked from one to the other and then escorted them over to a quiet corner.

'What are you up to, Simone?' he asked in a steely voice. 'I'm just putting her straight,' answered Simone.

'And I'd like to hear what she has to say,' said Lauren. 'I'm not scared of her, Jean-Luc.' Simone's face twisted into a smile. 'I'd like to hear the story she's dreamed up.'

The two girls faced each other. Lauren could see Jean-Luc didn't know what to do.

Simone's nails were digging into Lauren's arm. 'That's a divine dress you're wearing,' she said with sarcasm.

'Yes, I like it.' Lauren felt cool as if she'd dipped her face in an ice bucket. 'Yours too.'

She wanted to laugh. The whole thing was like a melodrama. One thing Lauren could do was stand up her herself.

With Simone still hanging on to her arm, they left the salon. A moment later, Simone pushed her through a doorway.

'Are you going to scratch my eyes out, Simone? I don't think so, because you've lost, haven't you? Jean-Luc told me about François and all your other indiscretions. He told me about this as well. You might be interested to know that so far nothing's happened between us—but it will. I don't need to sleep with a man to make him love me. Pity no-one told you that. It's not worth you fighting me for something you can't have. Well, where's this ring then?'

'Do you think I'd show you?' she asked.

'I thought that's what we came in here for?'

'You'll pay for this.'

'How? He won't believe a word you say. And I don't care what you do. I should give up, Simone. It's your birthday. You should be enjoying yourself.'

Lauren turned and looked in the mirror, then opened her bag, saw the roll of money and shut it again.

'I'm going back out now. This was really a useless exercise.' She passed Simone, who was looking very intimidating at that moment, opened the door and walked out.

Jean-Luc was outside fidgeting in the

corridor. 'What happened?'

'Nothing very much, but I think she's got the message.'

'Right. You didn't kill her, then?' They laughed, but she could see he was relieved. 'Shall we go back or do you want to go home? I think we've made our point.'

'No, thank you,' said Lauren. 'I'm just starting to enjoy myself.'

'Good girl,' he said, his eyes full of admiration.

After that, Simone left them alone. Lauren concluded she was a bully and she'd had to stand up to people before and Simone was no exception. They sat apart from the others and, soon became less the focus of the other guests' interest.

'She really thought she was getting engaged to you tonight?' Lauren asked when Simone re-appeared, perfect as ever. She ignored them both. 'She said you bought her a present.'

'I did—not recently. I'd been keeping it for a long time. I dropped it on the cabinet beside the bed when she was asleep with François. I hadn't the energy to knock the hell out of him. I couldn't care less any more.'

'Wow,' she said.

'Shall we dance?'

'Do you think we should?' She was looking at the small floor where only one other couple was dancing close.

'Yes, definitely.'

162

'Alright. Oh, what about my bag?'

'Just put it there in the chair.'

'The money,' she reminded him in an intense whisper.

'Most people here won't give a damn,' he said. 'It'll be fine.'

Looking apprehensive, she slipped it on the chair seat as far under the tablecloth as she could. He held out his hand and soon he was holding her so close that she was tingling all over. She could feel his body taut again hers and knew how much he wanted her. They were soon oblivious of the mixture of glances they were receiving.

More couples joined them in the candlelight. One or two of them nodded to Lauren and smiled, while several men manoeuvred close to him and congratulated him. All at once, it seemed as if they were among friends. Finally, they went back to the tables until the maitre d' announced dinner was served.

It was the most fantastic buffet Lauren had seen for a long time. Better than a five star hotel, she thought as Jean-Luc explained some of the courses as they walked along.

'I could get a taste for this,' she joked.

The threat of Simone was receding and she felt almost comfortable—that is, until she caught her rival watching her. She'd certainly not liked being humiliated, but Lauren was determined not to feel sorry for her.

'Entrées,' he said. 'Let me look. Fillet of solc, scallops gratineed, salmon mousse with capers, Endive salad with walnuts and Roquefort . . .'

'Stop, Jean-Luc,' she said. 'I'll just have this . . . and this . . .'

'Look at the desserts, cherie,' he whispered. 'Apricot crème caramel, Poire Belle-Helene. That's one of my favourites.'

An hour later, after they had danced again, she glanced at her watch. Gary wouldn't come now. She was surprised because Belleville was still there, chatting to guests and avoiding her and Jean-Luc. Lauren didn't blame him for being angry; Simone was his daughter after all.

Jean-Luc felt a little more relaxed. He had been worried when the two girls had gone to the Powder Room. He'd seen Simone in tempers and had to hold her off himself once or twice, yet Lauren didn't seem worried, which made him admire her even more. He loved everything about her. She was the perfect companion, feisty—she'd shown that in the way she tackled Simone—lovely but not conceited, intelligent . . . and half French. What more could he want?

And he wanted her completely. When they were dancing, all he desired was to take her to bed and he was convinced she wanted him too.

Only something that still worried him was why would someone want to kidnap her? It didn't make sense. He supposed that, sooner or later, the police would come up with the answer. He didn't want to consider things might go wrong.

Who'd have thought she would have been enjoying herself like she seemed to be tonight? He'd like to take her to his state room right now. He was imagining them making love . . .

She turned round. 'Penny for them?' she said.

'Oh, I was just thinking that perhaps we could sneak off and. I could show you my state room.'

'I'd like that,' she said, smiling and challenging him from under her lashes.

'Well, come on then,' he replied, taking her hand.

His heart was pounding, but right at that very moment, Simone walked into the middle of the room and called for attention. Everyone turned expectantly.

'I have an announcement to make,' she said, looking directly at Jean-Luc. 'I was hoping my father would make this speech, but this is not what he intended to say, but I'm sure you'll find it interesting nevertheless.'

She was looking at Lauren, who felt a little scared. Was this going to be the payback Simone had threatened?

Jean-Luc's hand slipped into Lauren's and squeezed it reassuringly. Then, he let it go and walked over to Simone.

'I should like to speak afterwards,' he

announced. They regarded each other. A few people clapped, then the salon became very quiet.

Lauren felt sick. Sense was overtaking euphoria. Why had she got involved with all this? These weren't her kind of people. She didn't want to doubt him, but could it be possible he'd been stringing her along? She closed her eyes for and moment and when she opened them Jean-Luc was looking straight at her.

His eyes seemed to be saying, *Don't worry.*

Simone looked round.

'As you all know, Jean-Luc and I have known each other since we used to play Kiss-Chase and I guess that's still going on for his part.' Jean-Luc frowned. 'We've had our share of ups and downs and tonight, my birthday, was going to be the best.'

She put her hand up and flashed an engagement ring. People started to clap, but she held up her hand. Jean-Luc glared, but still didn't make a move.

'Unfortunately, things don't always go to plan and he found it necessary to bring a guest with him. Look at her, over there!'

'That's enough, Simone,' Jean-Luc said in a hard voice.

'I haven't finished,' she said.

'You have.'

'I think I need to say this and you need to hear it.'

166

'You're wrong,' he said. 'The party's over.'

People were looking at each other and murmuring.

Simone shouted, 'This uninvited guest . . .'

'My guest, and my yacht,' said Jean-Luc.

Then Maurice Belleville stepped forward and put his hand on Jean-Luc's arm. He shook it off.

'Just a lovers' tiff, ladies and gentlemen.' Belleville's voice was placatory. He whispered something to Jean-Luc. People began to move away. Then Simone rushed over and grabbed her father's arm.

'No all of you, wait a minute, that girl over there has—' she said something under her breath. Her father stared then Jean-Luc and he were involved in a brief conversation.

'No, Lauren wouldn't do that,' said Jean-Luc.

Then Simone clutched his arm. 'Can you be sure of that?' Everyone was staring now. Simone turned. 'That girl is a thief! She stole my diamond pendant! The one Jean-Luc left by my bed this morning. I know she did it. Everyone here is a good friend of mine. Why would they want to do anything like that. They don't need to!'

'Lauren wouldn't and besides, she didn't know anything about your pendant.' Jean-Luc's voice was hard. 'Lauren?'

She went over to him. 'What diamond pendant? I don't know what you're talking about!' retorted Lauren.

'You're a liar. He told you he gave it to me, didn't he?'

'No, he didn't. How dare you?' Lauren was angry, but scared as well. 'Get your hands off me,' she said as Simone caught hold of her arm, digging her nails in as she did so.

Lauren pulled away and gathered her wrap round her shoulders. Her fingers were trembling.

'Father, call Security. Get them to search her bag,' Simone said icily.

Lauren couldn't bear the look on Jean-Luc's face and she began to cry in spite of herself as she turned towards the door and a burly man in black caught hold of her arm. She shook him off and turned to leave.

'Lauren, come back,' Jean-Luc shouted. 'You know she's lying. Don't go anywhere!' Lauren had no chance as her way was barred by another security man, his hand was on her shoulder bruising her skin and he spun her round, indicating she should hand over to her bag to him.

'I haven't done anything!' she cried.

Simone was running forward followed by Jean-Luc.

'I'll do it! I'll search it.' She tried to wrest the bag from Lauren but Jean-Luc pulled it away from her.

Simone had a nasty smile on her face. 'I want her bag searched first. I know everyone

168

else here, except her. Let him search it first. If there's nothing there, I'll apologise.'

'You'll do more than that,' said Lauren, her strength returning. 'I'll have you for slander!' They stared at each other. 'Fire away,' she said to the guard. 'Go on. Open it.'

The other guests were murmuring and nodding, craning their necks as he turned everything out on to the nearest table.

To Lauren's horror, a glittering diamond pendant on a chain tumbled out on the table followed by the roll of bank notes. The security man indicated the pendant, then held it up.

'Is this it?' he asked.

'Of course it is,' Simone said. 'It is, isn't it, Jean-Luc? You put it by my pillow when I was asleep this morning.'

Jean-Luc didn't speak and Lauren couldn't bear it. Not only had she been framed, but it was the way Simone implied that they were hunky-dory, that they shared each other's bed.

By then, the security man was counting the banknotes. The room was silent.

'Around seventeen thousand Euros,' said the man, holding up the roll. His narrowed eyes bored into Lauren, who heard the general gasp.

'Tell them, Jean-Luc. Tell them where we got the money.'

She implored him with her eyes. He seemed to be in shock. *He thinks I stole the pendant,* she thought.

'Give the cash to me,' Jean-Luc suddenly ordered. 'We've been playing the tables.'

The man nodded and handed it over.

'And the pendant?' hissed Simone. 'Can you explain that?'

'I'm sure she can, can't you, Lauren?' His face was grim.

'I've never seen the thing before! She must have put it there herself. No, wait, when we were dancing, I left my bag. Just there. You remember, don't you? You told me to put it there.'

Lauren's voice was urgent. She could see the odds were stacked against her and her one ally was looking at her as if he didn't know anything any more.

'Yes, she did leave it when we were dancing. Anyone could have got to it.'

People were nodding or shaking their heads. Then Maurice Belleville pushed through. He had his mobile in his hand.

'Jean-Luc, we have to call the police.'

'You can see he's shielding her,' urged Simone. 'He doesn't really believe it, do you? Poor Jean-Luc.'

'Lauren is not a thief!' he insisted.

'I'll call them,' said the security man. 'We're connected.'

Another security man had joined them. He was carrying a revolver. They spoke together briefly. The other one stood by the door, with his hand on his gun.

Lauren sunk into a chair, shaking. Why had she come? It was all terrible. She hadn't done anything, but when the police arrived, she'd have to tell them that her passport had been confiscated, making her look even guiltier. She couldn't even look at Jean-Luc.

The she felt an arm round her shaking shoulders.

'Don't cry, Lauren, please, we'll get to the bottom of this. I believe you.' She didn't answer.

As he stood there, trying to comfort her, he was thinking it was impossible Lauren could have known about the diamond pendant. He racked his brains as to what he'd told her about finding Simone in bed with his yacht master. He was sure he hadn't mentioned a pendant, so why had he any doubts that Simone had framed her?

He hated himself for even thinking of it and he despised Simone now more than ever, because it had caused him to doubt a girl he had begun to fall in love with, a girl he'd thought meant something to him for the first time in his life—and he hated himself for even entertaining the thought that Lauren might be a thief.

'I'm going to wring Simone's neck,' he said to Lauren. 'I promise.' She didn't answer and in one horrible moment, he knew he'd blown it with her and that she'd probably never trust him again. He'd behaved like a spineless fool.

He looked up at the guests who had called for their wraps and coats and who were preparing to leave.

'Stop,' he said. 'All of you, please. This is my yacht and I am going to get to the bottom of this. I'm going to find out who's framed Lauren and if it's one of you, then you'll pay for it. I advise you not to talk about this outside or you could find yourselves in court. Just one thing, you know now why I decided to split up with Miss Belleville. I expect her and Maurice to stay put. I have plenty to say to them. Good night.'

There was a hum of surprised and anxious voices as well as an immediate flurry of activity as wraps and coats were brought in by the staff and handed over to their owners.

Lauren still sat, staring at nothing. She was thinking that the police would be here soon and she was going to have no defence, except for Jean-Luc who had shaken her faith in him seriously. Simone, holding her father's arm, was seated by the bar, throwing occasional triumphant glances in the direction of her rival. While Jean-Luc still stood, his face impassive, waiting for the arrival of the police, the security guard had disappeared.

After all the guests had left, Maurice Belleville looked at his watch. 'Where the hell are the police?' he asked. Then they heard the sound of a heavy engine. 'That's them! Now we'll get this sorted out . . . what the hell?'

A hooded man carrying a revolver and supported by two others also dressed in black with only their eyes showing through balaclavas burst into the salon. They were carrying weapons which were pointed at the four of them.

'Down!' they shouted, 'All of you!'

*   *   *

A few minutes later, a terrified Lauren and Simone were sitting facing each other as their mouths were taped by one of the men. The other was tying their ankles and their arms behind them. Maurice Belleville and Jean-Luc were lying face downwards on the floor, guarded by the third.

Then the door opened to reveal a man in a black suit. He was accompanied by two more heavies, carrying the same Kalashnikovs as the others.

The suited man stood over Jean-Luc and said, 'Nice to make your acquaintance, Hilarie. I'm looking forward to getting to know you.' Then he turned to Belleville. 'I won't say it's nice to make yours, you double-crossing bastard. You and I have a lot to say to each other.' He kicked Belleville, who yelped in agony.

Simone was struggling. The man knelt down in front of her and grabbing her chin, forced her to look at him. 'You're just as pretty as he said you were. François . . . You know him? He's feeding the fishes now.' She went completely still. 'But not before he told us you would be able to give us a lot of help.'

'What do you want?' muttered Jean-Luc, his voice muffled.

One of the heavies was about to kick him, but the man who seemed to be the boss held up his hand.

'No! We need him to be fit. He has work to do. We'll take the old guy first. Search Hilarie's pockets.' He turned to Jean-Luc. 'Keep still,' he warned, 'Don't try to do anything stupid, or we might blow your head off or . . .' he turned to Lauren. 'Or have some fun with your girlfriend.

'A pity you got mixed up with Mr Grey,' he directed his words to Lauren, who flinched. 'You're his secretary, aren't you? You had plenty of fight in you the other day, but you won't get away this time. Who knows where you'll end up, unless you tell us what we want to know. You'd make a pretty little meal for the fishes, but I wouldn't like that. We could be friends. My men tell me you're a bad girl . . . Stealing diamonds, eh? Tsk, tsk.'

His laugh was sinister.

'Hey, boss,' said the heavy, holding up the notes. The man grinned and made a gesture to the man to throw it over. He packed it into his pocket.

'You're expensive, Lauren. What did you do

174

for that? Would you do it for me?' He thrust his face near to her, 'But I haven't the time right now . . . pity. But there's always later.'

Then his heavy handed him Jean-Luc's mobile phone. He stood, fiddling with the buttons, then looked up and nodded.

'Get rid of it,' he ordered. The man dropped it and stamped on it. 'Tie him up like the rest of them. Pull the old man out, we'll question him first. No-one takes what's mine! And spread them out. We don't want any heroics.'

The heavy nodded as he tied Jean-Luc's hands behind him. Lauren watched in helpless horror as the first man bent over a moaning Belleville and hoisted the jeweller up. A moment later, he dragged them out of the salon, one by one and down into a smaller room.

All was silent for a while, until they heard an agonised scream in the distance. Simone began to cry quietly, but then the lights flickered and went out and with horror they felt the yacht move. They were under way.

A moment later, a surprising thing happened. The guard went and stood over Jean-Luc. 'I'm not doing this out of the goodness of my heart. Any funny stuff and I'll blow a hole in your head—and the girls. It's for our mutual benefit, you understand. You'll get no second chance.'

Jean-Luc nodded, looking at the gun.

'One peep from you girls and you'll get it.'

He turned to Jean-Luc again. 'They're going to want you up there in a minute. They need a pilot since they've done for François. If they come in, I'll say you were having a fit. Agreed?'

Jean-Luc nodded. Then, the man stooped and tore off the tape enough to free Jean-Luc's mouth. Lauren felt hope. This man was going to help them—for whatever reason. She looked at Jean-Luc who was moistening his lips and swallowing as if he was trying to get his voice back.

'I want to know where the jewels are hidden. It'll save us all a lot of trouble—and the girls a lot of pain,' said their captor.

Jean-Luc stared over at the two of them. 'And what will it do for you?' asked Jean-Luc.

Lauren was horrified. Was Jean-Luc smuggling jewels?

'Don't ask questions!' He pointed the gun.

'I don't know what jewels you're referring to,' Jean-Luc said, 'But if you let us go I'll pay you more than any jewels are worth.'

'No deal.'

'No honour amongst thieves then,' Jean-Luc replied.

'They'll get it out of you—or the girls,' the man said. 'So be it.' He taped Jean-Luc's mouth again.

Simone was struggling and nodding violently. He went over. 'And what's the matter with you then? You want to speak?'

176

She kept nodding. He went close to her. 'Are you trying to tell me you know where they are?' She nodded.

'Well,' he said, 'Someone has sense. It better not be a trick or you'll be for it.'

The lights went on. He took out his mobile and spoke. 'I've got something for you . . . yes, one of the women.'

Jean-Luc was struggling again. The man went over and kicked him. 'You had your chance. You won't have another.'

He turned to Simone. 'One way or another, you're dead if you're lying.' She nodded. He was staring at her with appreciation in his eyes, when the door opened and two others came in. Their captor indicated Simone. Together, they dragged her up from the floor.

'This better be good,' they said. 'Otherwise you'll go the same way as your old man.'

Lauren began to shake. As they took Simone away, Jean-Luc was trying to drag himself over to reach her. She knew he was trying to comfort her even though their captor was watching. Strangely enough, he didn't try to stop Jean-Luc as he rolled his way painfully over the floor towards Lauren, speaking to her only with his eyes.

Finally, he made it and soon they were huddled together. Lauren thought, If I'm going to die, I want it to be with him. I knew he isn't a crook and I'm sure he doesn't think I am either.

CHAPTER EIGHT

Simone screamed out as they reached the bridge and rushed towards her father, who was lying motionless and bleeding. He moaned when he saw her.

'Don't kill her please, she knows nothing.'

'What have you done to him?' shouted Simone.

'Taught him a lesson,' said the man who was evidently the boss and was sitting beside the man who had taken François' place as yacht master. 'I'm satisfied he doesn't know where our property is hidden, although he double-crossed us with François, which he's now discovered was very unwise. I'm considering throwing him over the side, but that might change.' His eyes were strafing Simone. 'So you're the one who knows where our property is? The girl who was messing with François?'

His eyes travelled all over her from her creased and torn silk sheath upwards to her half-exposed breasts.

'Nice dress,' he said. 'François told where he hid our package, did he? You may be interested to know he sold you out, darling, when he was pleading for his life. But he was one of our own and he broke the code of conduct. He had to go.'

'Why didn't you ask me then instead of

starting with my father?' She went and knelt by him, but was dragged away. 'You're brutes!' she said, lifting her chin, the old Simone coming back. 'If I tell you, will you let us go—my father and Jean-Luc?'

'Your ex-lover? And the other girl?'

'You can kill her for all I care!'

The man grinned. 'A woman after my own heart. But I wonder if Hilarie would agree.' He sniffed. 'I have no interest in lovers' tiffs, but if you're lying, you'll both end up in the sea.'

'I'm not. He showed me where the package was himself, but I'm not going to do it unless you promise to let us go.'

'Bargaining? You have nothing to bargain with. Like your father, you'll show us when you're in enough pain. Hopefully, it's not going to be like that. I would hate to . . .' he breathed in deeply, '. . . damage you.'

As they took Simone out, he leaned back in his chair, swivelled round and spoke on his mobile.

*   *   *

Lauren and Jean-Luc jumped as the man's phone rang. Their captor put it to his ear and grinned.

'Thanks boss.' He turned to them. 'The hunt is underway. Let's hope the girl knows what she's doing. You have ten minutes,' he said to Jean-Luc. 'Then he wants you up on the bridge. You're still useful to us . . . but you,' he said, turning to Lauren, '. . . haven't anything to bargain with, have you?'

The man was right. She knew nothing and she could see no way out of her predicament. It was torture. It was no good regretting she'd ever come to the South of France with Gary, but what she most regretted was that she might never see Jean-Luc again when he was taken away. She began to cry and all he could do was press against her for comfort.

Then something amazing happened. Their captor walked over to her and she flinched, but the next moment, he took off one glove deliberately and caught hold of her shoulder. She tried to huddle against Jean-Luc for protection, then stopped moving, wide-eyed, as she saw the large Russian diamond ring with the two unusual claw hands sparkling at her on the man's finger.

She looked up at him, couldn't believe it, and her urgent eyes asked, *Paul?*

He nodded, crouched down beside them and whispered. 'Yes, it's me! All you need to know is I'm on your side. It's going to be alright. Sorry, I have to make this look real. They're on their way.' They could hear footsteps approaching. 'Just play along and don't give me away. Both your lives depend on it.'

As the door opened, Paul slapped Lauren's face lightly and she cried out. He kicked Jean-

Luc as he was dragged to his feet.

'You might as well take her too,' Paul said. The men looked doubtful. 'It doesn't make sense me being down here with her on our own. I might do something I'd regret.'

They laughed. 'What about the boss?' asked one.

'I'll square it with him. I'm in his good books.'

As Lauren was dragged up a corridor behind Jean-Luc, she'd begun to hope, although she couldn't believe it. Paul was an undercover agent! It seemed ridiculously impossible.

Then the things she'd seen and heard working for Gary and the two men's strange relationship and mystery visits were all beginning to come into focus and make sense. West Africa. Diamonds. She'd seen the TV programmes about diamonds that came from war zones in Africa and were sold illegally to fund terrorist war efforts against legitimate governments and sometimes those countries that weren't recognised internationally. The men who were holding them might be a gang like that! Now she knew how dangerous they were and if they had been double-crossed and Maurice Belleville had been involved, maybe Gary had too! Where was he? Why wasn't Paul with him? Maybe they'd got him and he'd suffered the same as this François they kept talking about. She felt cold with fear.

That must have been why they tried to abduct her because they thought that she could tell them what Gary was up to. Then Jean-Luc had intervened. At least he knew nothing about their missing hoard, which they seemed to think was stashed in the yacht. It would have been a perfect cover.

When Jean-Luc told her that Simone's lover was François, she hadn't been surprised. The girl was ruthless as Lauren had just found out. She'd stoop to anything with money in it. But why did François tell her? Perhaps he thought he'd steal the loot and run away with her.

I wish he had, thought Lauren. What if he'd been lying? What would happen to them all if she didn't find the stuff. But Simone said she knew where it was. Lauren shivered. Jean-Luc couldn't be involved! A little doubt had crept into her mind earlier, which she had tried to squash; that maybe he knew whatever they were looking for was hidden on his boat. Now her heart told her that he wasn't like that, that he had enough money of his own not to risk his life for illegal diamonds. They were stones he dealt with every day. All that she hoped for now was that he didn't know about Belleville's dealings with the gang.

As for Paul, he'd always managed to steer her out of trouble, why shouldn't this time be different—except that there were a lot more of them to tackle than Gary! He must have back-up, she said to herself.

As she stared down at the polished deck, she remembered how beautiful she'd thought the yacht was when she first saw it. Tonight it seemed lonely and menacing as they headed back towards the salon. She thought of the Mediterranean, dark enough to swallow up their bodies, and became really scared as negative thoughts threatened to overtake her brief, rising hope. What was going to happen to them?

Lauren struggled to be positive. *You need to keep focused, Lauren,* otherwise you'll go to pieces, she told herself. *Keep your head. You might be able to help!*

It felt like a route march. How long did Jean-Luc say the yacht was? It seemed like miles as she stumbled along, knocking her jutting elbows into things as they passed. Her arms felt numb from being constricted for so long and her face was sore and aching where the tape was burning into her skin.

Paul had caught them up and was hustling her on all the way. She kept remembering what he'd just said. *We have to make this look real.* Then ridiculous thoughts began to take over. Maybe he's a liar and when he knows where the stash is, he'll kill us too! She fought against the doubts. If he had, he wouldn't have revealed himself. Or would he? It was agony!

The door opened to reveal a changed bridge. All traces of the glittering guests had gone and it looked like a military operations

HQ with kit bags, guns and ammunition. The man in black was sitting at the helm beside another of the gang, who was consulting a chart spread out before him.

This is where I was expecting to have a good time, not a living nightmare, thought Lauren.

The gang boss was staring at her and she looked at the floor. He came over and brushed her face all over with his hand, then jerked her chin upwards. She tried to brave it out.

'This one's even prettier than the blonde,' he said, strafing her body with his eyes. Lauren looked at Jean-Luc, who looked agonised. 'I could have some fun with you.'

Lauren cried out as Paul whipped the tape off.

'You've done a good job,' the boss said to Paul. 'I'm pleased I took you on.' He smirked. 'Though being a gentleman, I don't usually employ mercenaries. They're too much trouble. Look at him, ladies and gentlemen. A killing machine. Just make sure you keep making him happy.'

'Thank you, sir.' Paul saluted and the man grinned.

'He's also a technical wizard.' Paul remained at attention. The man laughed and slapped him hard on the chest. Jean-Luc shot a glance at him, then away.

Lauren breathed in to calm herself. If the boss suspected Paul, they'd all be done for.

So that's what he was . . . a mercenary. It

figured. She thought of the scar she'd noticed, deep under his hairline. He must have taken a bullet in some conflict or other. Perhaps he was ex-special forces. Her dad had told her about the things they did. Her hopes lifted. If he was still one of them, then he'd have back-up—and they'd storm the boat—but would the hostages survive? They often didn't. She didn't want to think of that, so she just kept her eyes fixed on Jean-Luc. It made her feel better.

'What do you think of this one, eh?' added the boss, indicating Lauren. Paul looked her up and down and grinned.

A second later, the boss struck him hard in the face. Only a muscle quivered in his cheek and he still stood and erect. The boss smiled, 'Hey, tough guy. I like that.' He turned to Lauren. 'How would you like to be handed over to him?'

Lauren swallowed back the bile in her throat, then they heard a hum beneath them.

'The bilge pump,' said Jean-Luc.

'Nasty in there,' said the boss, 'Full of little fishes and who knows what else.' He turned to Jean-Luc, whose expression was a mixture of anger and loathing as he looked at him. 'You,' he said, 'Little, rich boy. You were getting too greedy.'

'Whatever stuff is stashed on my yacht,' Jean-Luc's voice was ice-cold. 'I'm not responsible for it.'

Lauren held her breath. What would they

do to him if he stood up to them?

'You've courage,' the boss said, 'But wait until we have a go at your girlfriend.'

'Touch her, you'll have me to answer to. Where's Simone?'

'The Belleville blonde's on a treasure hunt.'

'And Belleville? You like torturing old men and women?'

The gang boss jerked his head and Paul hit Jean-Luc in the stomach so hard that he doubled up and fell to the deck.

Lauren screamed and tried to run to him, but Paul held her off, his arms round her body. There was no consolation in his arms, in spite of what she knew. He seemed oblivious to her pain. The sensible part of her knew why, but all she wanted was to scream and shout at him, *Why don't you do something? Why are you hurting us like this? Please help us! Now!*

The boss approached Jean-Luc, who was trying to get up.

'That's for your insolence. You wanted to know about Belleville. He's still alive—just. We've been nice to him. He's in one of the state rooms, but unfortunately if his daughter doesn't come up with the goods, he won't last long.'

'You're sick,' shouted Jean-Luc. He was still clutching his stomach. 'What about her?' Jean-Luc gestured to Lauren.

'You're safe, Hilarie. Your job is reading the charts. Don't concern yourself with your girlfriend. I'll look after her.'

Jean-Luc was dragging himself to his feet now and looking at Paul with hatred in his eyes. Lauren realised that every blow he took was part of the authenticity; Paul had to be a brute.

'Why the charts? We have GPS?' Jean-Luc said.

'Had, is the word, thanks to our tecchie.' He indicated Paul. 'Do you think we're idiots to let all the world know where we are? That's your job.'

Lauren's hopes were up again. If Paul had disabled the GPS, he'd be able to put it together again. Or maybe he hadn't really? But she didn't know anything about global positioning. Maybe the others could tell if it was on or not?

'Where are we headed?' asked Jean-Luc, on his feet now.

'You'll know soon enough, when we get our stuff back.'

'She's not ocean-going any more,' retorted Jean-Luc.

'Don't give me that,' the man snarled. 'This old girl has the speed. That's why we chose her. She's trustworthy—like I was told you were. You've good credit in Monte.'

'And I'll be missed! Have you thought of that? They'll be looking for me—and the police will be looking for Lauren.'

She stared at him. Why did he say that?

Why did he tell them about her?

'I'm still not convinced you knew nothing about the old man's double-crossing dealings, Hilarie. We don't like being shafted, and, as for Little Miss Jewel Thief here, it sounds as if we have something in common.'

'I'm not a thief,' she said. 'And I've nothing in common with you!' She saw Jean-Luc shake his head at her and Paul's eyes swivel in her direction, saying *Don't be brave! Don't antagonise him!* But at that moment, she couldn't help it.

'That's a pity. It would have made it so much more fun you being a bad girl. Next you'll tell me that you knew nothing about your boss and our diamonds.'

'I didn't—until I got mixed up in all this!' Her brain was working crazily. Gary and diamonds! The stupid idiot getting mixed up in this? Her bravado melted as Paul walked to her.

'Keep your mouth shut,' he said, 'Or you'll get this.' He made a fist and his eyes warned her silently.

'Alright,' she said. For the first time since they came on to the bridge, she could see a momentary softness in his eyes.

'You keep away from her,' shouted Jean-Luc. 'If you want to take it out on someone, I'm your man. As for you . . .'

'Jean-Luc, please!' cried Lauren, knowing there was no need to be brave, but she knew how he felt and loved him for it.

The boss held up his hand. 'Enough! We want him fit enough to navigate. You're scaring the girl, Hilarie, but she'll be a lot more scared if you don't do what you're told. If the blonde doesn't come back soon with the stash, you'll be going on a detailed tour and when you come back, both of them won't be here. They'll be joining Daddy in the state room. That's when the fun begins.' He grinned.

Lauren closed her eyes. Not being close to Jean-Luc was a terrifying thought. He couldn't help her, but she needed him to be with her. She was desperate for another reassuring glimpse from the old Paul, but knew that if he did, they were all finished.

Inwardly she kept on thinking, *What are you waiting for? When are you going to do something?* It was agony, but she kept pushing away the panic, knowing he must have some plan.

Then the boss man's mobile rang. He answered and listened for a moment.

'Bring her up!' he said and then turned to Jean-Luc. 'Pity, but it seems your ex has been playing a game with us. Leading us on a wild goose chase as the English say. I don't like that.'

Jean-Luc looked at Lauren, who had started trembling involuntarily. A few minutes later, the girl who was pushed through the door was unrecognisable as Simone; she was wet through, shivering and sobbing.

'Have you been for a swim?' said the boss.

'We were only having a bit of fun, sir, when she couldn't find the stuff,' said one of the men who was in a wet suit.

'I won't ask you what you did to her, but it wasn't in my orders. Where did she take you?'

'She said it was in the bilges, but searching them is a dry dock job.'

'Do you think I don't know that?' he growled. He approached Simone, who shrank back. 'You trying to make an idiot of me?'

'No,' she sobbed. 'François showed me. He said the package was down there.'

The boss shook his head. 'You little airhead. You were playing for time, weren't you?'

'I wasn't, I wasn't! I've never been deep down in the yacht before. I don't know how . . .' Simone was gabbling.

Lauren couldn't help it; she broke away and ran over to her to put her arms round her. Simone was inconsolable, broken, and she felt ice-cold.

'She's freezing to death—get her a blanket!'

'This isn't a hotel,' the boss retorted. He looked the angriest Lauren had seen so far.

'They tried to kill me!' Simone appealed to Lauren. 'Don't let them. He said it was there! They . . . the sea . . . I've been in the sea . . .' She retched and Jean-Luc looked agonised.

'Two days pay!' snarled the boss.

'We thought the stuff might be dangling

190

over, like he'd hung it over the side so we . . .'
The man broke off as the boss jerked his head
to Paul, who went over and punched him hard.

'Did you make sure?' he said to the man in
the wet suit.

'Yes, Boss. I went along the water line.
Nothing.'

'Break them up,' he ordered, indicating the
girls.

Simone screamed. 'Don't touch me. Don't!'
as Lauren was prised off her.

'Nobody's going to touch you, looking like
that,' replied the boss ominously. 'Take her to
the guest state and get her clothes off. She can
go talk to Daddy. The other woman as well.'

'Oh, my God, Jean-Luc,' cried Lauren. She
saw Paul's impassive face and hated him at
that moment. Jean-Luc sprang forward and
Paul tripped him, leaving him sprawled on
deck.

Jean-Luc staggered to his feet. Lauren saw
to her horror that he was bleeding from his
forehead. She couldn't rush to him, because
Paul was blocking the way. Lauren began to
cry. She'd kept back the tears so long and now
she was exhausted.

'Take them away,' growled the boss man.' I
can't stand all this blubbering.'

A heavy approached Lauren and pushed
her in the direction of Simone. They stood
together, shivering while Jean-Luc put his
hand to his head and wiped off the blood.

'I'll find what you want if it's on this yacht, I know it through and through, and when I do, will you let them go—Belleville and the two girls? I'll take you wherever you're going.'

'Spoken like a true gentleman,' the boss said. 'But I don't do bargains. However, I appreciate the sentiment. You,' he said to Paul, 'Take him and the frogman—and don't come back without what I want. If you need more manpower you know where it is. You,' he said to the other heavy, 'Take them to the state room. And don't touch, or you'll be feeding the fishes. Guard them, nothing else!'

'Move,' ordered Paul and with a swift glance at Lauren, he lifted the Kalashnikov and began to push Jean-Luc to the door.

'Hilarie,' called the boss, 'They'll be safe— at least until you come back.'

*   *   *

If everything wasn't so terrifying, Lauren would have noticed the guest room was as sumptuous as the best hotel, but all she her attention focused on was Maurice Belleville lying on the floor.

'Is he dead?' wailed Simone. 'Is Daddy dead?'

'Nah, he's just out of it,' said the man. 'But he could be on the way.'

'What did you do to him?' shouted Lauren. The man shook his head and held up his hands. 'You coward,' she snapped.

Simone was pulling at her arm. 'No, no, don't upset him. He'll kill you.' Lauren could see she was terrified of the brute.

'I don't think so,' said Lauren, 'You go to your dad, then we'll get you warm.'

The man was following her every move with his eyes. Lauren was thinking that if something happened to Jean-Luc and if Paul's team, or whoever he was working with, didn't show up in time, she didn't care if he killed her. The thought of what that evil man up on the bridge was going to do them would be far worse than death!

'I hope you're not going to stand there watching us,' she turned on the heavy. 'We can't fly out of here can we? We haven't any phones. Give us some privacy.'

'No way.' The man stood his ground, strafing her body with hungry eyes. She had to be strong.

'What did your boss say he'd do to you if you touched us.'

'I'm not going to.'

'I'll tell him you did unless you get out.'

'You bitch!' he said, lifting his gun.

'You'll be dead as well as me if you use that,' she replied, shaking inside. 'Now, get out and give us some privacy.'

The man backed away. She could see he was turning over the possibilities, but her ruse worked. A moment later, he turned and walked out of the door.

He stopped on the threshold. 'The phone lines have been ripped out,' he said, 'Don't try anything.'

'Would I?' she said, slamming the door in his face. At that moment, all she wanted to do was to scream and sob like Simone, but instead, she went over to her. She was bent over, kneeling by her father and crying.

'That'll do no good. Move back,' Lauren said. She pulled her up and Simone flopped against the bed, watching while Lauren took her place. Belleville's breathing was shallow and he had heavy bruises to his face. His grey-haired chest was exposed which showed he'd taken a body battering too. She hadn't any medical experience except a First Aid course years ago and she dredged through her memory of it for something useful.

'Help me,' she called to Simone. 'Help me to put him in the recovery position.'

Simone obeyed, but it took a little while, she was so afraid and it was like talking to a child. What had happened to the old Simone? What had they done to her? Lauren supposed she was in shock.

Lauren propped Belleville's back with pillows in case he rolled back again. There was nothing else she could do. He needed an ambulance, which he wasn't going to get.

She straightened up and took Simone's arm. 'Come on, Simone. Let's get you out that wet dress as soon as possible.'

She led Simone to a chair then looked round. She could see a door across the room and opened it. The shower room. She didn't care about anything at that moment except getting under the shower and washing away the touch of them all. She ran the bath and went back to Simone. All she could do now was look after her. Whatever the girl had done to her in the past, she was a broken woman now. Lauren helped Simone peel off her sopping wet dress, which smelled of dirty sea water and she shuddered at the thought of what must have happened to her.

'You have the bath. I'll use the shower. Come on,' she said. 'We'll get through this together.'

All at once, Simone looked at her with eyes red from crying and said, 'Do you hate me? I . . . I put the pendant in your bag.'

'I know you did, but that doesn't matter now. What we have to do is survive—and we will. Remember, we have Jean-Luc. He'll get us out of this.'

Lauren didn't elaborate. She wasn't going to mention Paul to Simone. The state she was in she was likely to do anything and Lauren still didn't really trust her.

Lauren was soon standing under the shower, wishing she was able to wash this terrible night away with the water. Wrapping herself in a huge towel when she'd done, she approached the bath. Simone looked as if she were asleep in it. Whether she'd made any attempt to wash, Lauren didn't know, but she concluded that with all the expensive body wash she'd poured in, the job would be done, so she fetched a towel.

'Simone,' she said, 'Come on. You have to get out and sleep for a bit, but you can't sleep in the bath or you'll drown.'

At the word drown, Simone opened her eyes and stared at her. She looked terrified and Lauren helped her out and wrapped both Simone and herself in thick towelling robes.

They fell on the bed together and lay there. Lauren kept thinking about Jean-Luc and what he was doing now. Maybe when he couldn't find the jewels, they'd do the same thing to him as they done to Simone. She was pretty sure now that the men had pretended to drown her. If they had, they'd done a good job of it. This time they might really to do it to the man she cared for more than anyone else in the world.

Lauren couldn't even close her eyes although she was exhausted; she was too tense, every little noise scared her.

Simone stirred after about half an hour and looked round. 'This is my bedroom,' she said unexpectedly.

Lauren couldn't think of any reply. She looked down at Belleville, who hadn't moved. Maybe he's dead now, she thought. Internal injuries. What are we going to do? Panic was returning and she had to think of something to do.

'What's that door over there? Your walk-in wardrobe?'

'That's Jean-Luc's.'

'Bedroom?'

Simone nodded. Adjoining rooms, thought Lauren, but all she could think of now was how much she would have given to see him come through that door.

She got up and went to the outer door they'd come through which had a spyhole. The man with the gun was still guarding them. She hurried over to Jean-Luc's door and tried it warily—it opened! She could see clothes scattered everywhere and drawers turned upside down as well as wardrobes hanging open. It flickered into her mind that if the outer door of his room wasn't locked then maybe they'd be able to get out of the corridor . . . but what about the armed guard?

Lauren crept over to the door into the corridor and tried the handle. The door wasn't locked. She crept back over the plush carpet into the adjoining suite.

'Come on, Simone,' she said. 'We have to pull ourselves together and help ourselves. Get dressed. Quickly.'

CHAPTER NINE

The first place Jean-Luc thought that the diamonds might be stashed was the screw of the propeller. He had seen screws stripped by Customs men before when they were searching for contraband, but it all depended how long François had been planning to double-cross them—and it needed to be done in dry dock. Paul must know that too if he was a policeman.

Jean-Luc was in the front, followed by the man in the wet suit, followed by Paul. Both were walking behind him and didn't speak. Jean-Luc stopped but the man pushed him on.

Paul said, 'Wait! See what he wants.' The man stopped. Jean-Luc turned and he saw Paul indicate he keep him talking.

'What have you stopped for?' asked his captor.

'I'm thinking that the stash might be in the screw. Where would you hide a fortune's worth of diamonds?'

'How should I know?' growled the man. 'What are you playing at?'

'I'm being honest,' replied Jean-Luc. 'The problem is yachts are usually in dry dock to search for smuggled diamonds.'

'How d'you know we're looking for diamonds?' spat the man.

'What else costs a fortune? Uranium or

polonium come to that. Do you know how much that costs? That Russian in London was killed by that. Horrible death . . .' Jean-Luc prattled on. 'He took days to die. I saw his photo in the paper . . .' Jean-Luc continued. He daren't look at Paul, so he fixed his eyes on his captor, holding his attention completely.

A moment later, the man suddenly fell backwards. Paul was pulling a narrow cord round his neck tighter and tighter and his eyes were bulging.

Jean-Luc stood back, sickened. He'd never seen a man die like that before; in a road accident once, but never murdered.

The man's hands were scrabbling against his throat trying to release the cord, then gradually he slumped to the floor.

'Come on,' said Paul, 'help me.' Together they dragged him under the companionway and covered him with a tarpaulin.

'One down,' said Paul. 'Four to go. You've got to do something now. We haven't much time. If I know the big boss, he'll be wanting to leave the bridge soon. I need to get up there and restore the GPS. I've a team standing by. Don't ask any more questions but do exactly as I say. Here.'

He withdrew a pistol and handed it over.

'A Glock.' Jean-Luc turned it over.

'Have you used the gun before?'

'Not one of these. Only a rifle. Trap shooting.'

'I should have known,' replied Paul. 'Right, listen. I'm going to call the heavy who's got the girls and lure him down here.'

'You're going to kill him too?'

'If I have to, but he might see sense.'

Jean-Luc realised the last sentence was nonsense; he was going to dispatch the man as easily as he did the other. He told himself Paul was a professional killer and he could never be that, but whatever happened, they all had to get out of this mess and Paul was their only hope.

'He'll still be guarding the state room door now. He'll jump to it if I call him down here. If he isn't still there, I'll have to improvise.' Jean-Luc nodded and Paul continued, 'I want him off your back because you're going to your bedroom. The outside and internal door to your suite is open and you need to get to them before the boss does. I'm going to call him now, but I'll give you some time. Five minute tops.'

He called, then gave the man rapid instructions.

'He's there, alright. If the boss is not on the bridge, we have a problem. We'll have to let the creep get to them.'

'No way.' Jean-Luc looked grim.

'No stupid heroics. I have to get on the bridge and re-enable the GPS. You won't be able to handle the boss if you go in there cold—unless you want to die—but if you're

200

waiting for him inside, that's different. If the best happens and he's still on the bridge, I'll get him off there, tell him we've got a good lead on the stash's whereabouts and the other two are still helping you. By the way, you're supposed to be looking for two kilos of uncut stones. I'll say they're having to break up some of the galley area. He'll trust me, I've been working for him a long time. I know how he works and he can't wait to get his hands on the girls—and he mustn't. Then it's up to you. You know this boat.

'I'll also deal with the heavy who's playing pilot,' Paul went on. 'Now, my orders are to keep the boss alive, so I don't want you doing a Tom Cruise on me and blasting his head off when he gets in their room, got it? When he turns up in the bedroom where you'll be waiting for him, disable him, aim for arms or legs, no head shots.'

Jean-Luc took it all in. The thought of that man with his hands all over the girls made him sick.

'With luck I'll have done my bit then on the bridge and then I'll back you up. But it's vital I get the GPS working.'

'Has the boss got a key to the state room? I imagine the heavy will lock the door.'

'Yep, he's got a full set of keys. By the way, they shot François then chucked him in the drink.'

Jean-Luc shook his head. 'I didn't like the

man but . . .'

'These arc vcry bad guys. The other thing you don't want to know, but what I have to tell you is, if the GPS is switched on again before the agreed place, we'll have two or three fast speedboats on our tail, stuffed with nasties. We want our lads out here first. Otherwise, we'll be fighting a whole bloody army. That's why I've been waiting.' He checked his watch. 'We haven't much time. Ten minutes tops.

'Got it,' repeated Jean-Luc, checking the gun.

'No need to check, she's loaded. By the way, sorry for the kicking, but it was necessary. Now, d'you think you can do it?'

'No problem.' Jean-Luc intended to get back to his state room at all costs. Paul had his cell phone ready. 'Ok?' Jean-Luc nodded, 'Go for it. The heavy will be nearly down here now. Keep out of his way. Good luck.'

Jean-Luc was off and praying that the sleazeball on the bridge hadn't beaten him to it. Thinking of what he might do to Lauren made him sick and as for Simone, whatever she had done she didn't deserve this and he felt pity for what she'd been through as he would have done for any woman.

It felt strange to be handling a gun. *Disable him.* The words rang in his head. It wouldn't be his choice—if Jean-Luc had his own way about it, the pig wouldn't ever be able to mess with women again—but he knew Paul was right. The man needed to be tried and put away for life.

Keep your head, Jean-Luc, he told himself over and over again as he crept towards the stateroom, getting off the main corridor and taking the most circuitous way possible so that he wouldn't be spotted by the girls' guard.

He hated diamonds and everything to do with them. They'd brought him wealth, but not his father's happiness nor his. The only place he wanted to see a diamond was sparkling on Lauren's finger. He was looking for a different life untainted by whatever shady things Belleville had done or made his father do. He had to pull this off. He'd never shot anyone before, but now their survival was at stake.

As Jean-Luc approached the corridor leading to the bedrooms, he was sweating. He took off his shoes in case the man heard— that's if he were inside. He wiped his hand on his trousers; he didn't want the pistol missing its target. He paused at the end of the corridor leading to the state rooms and flattened himself against the wall. Praying, he ducked out to see if the corridor was empty. It was.

Jean-Luc was past praying that the boss wouldn't be with the girls already. He listened at both doors. Nothing. God, don't let them be dead, he thought. Slowly, he turned the handle of his bedroom and, with the gun ready, he pushed the door. It only yielded a little. *Why did I make the carpets that deep?* was the stupid thought that came into his head.

*   *   *

Lauren and Simone had already decided what to do ten minutes earlier.

'We have to try and help ourselves,' said Lauren. 'If you won't help, I'm going to leave you. I'm not going to die on this boat.' Simone had stared at her as if she didn't understand. 'If we don't get off here, we're going to die,' insisted Lauren.

'But what about Daddy?'

'He'll die anyway if we don't get him to hospital. You know this boat, Simone—where could we hide? Think! That beast will be coming down here soon and he's going to— Oh, never mind, just tell me where we could hide until P—' She almost let it slip.

'There's a life-boat,' said Simone. 'I know where it is.'

'And you could find it in the dark?' Simone nodded. 'Right. I know what we'll do. We'll go into Jean-Luc's room. Then we'll go over to the door and both throw something heavy into this room.' Simone looked blank and Lauren was frustrated.

'Something heavy—what? Vase, that vase,' she grabbed it. 'You take the other.' She thrust it into Simone's hands. 'Come on. We get over to the door and then we throw them into this room. The man outside will think something's

204

happened to us. By then, we'll have made a run for it. We have to do it. I'm not waiting here to be raped by some sicko.'

'I'm coming, too, Lauren,' Simone said. It was the first time she'd ever used Lauren's name. Holding the vases, they moved together towards the door to Jean-Luc's's bedroom.

*   *   *

Once Jean-Luc was in, he looked round and towards the adjoining door to the guest suite, which was slightly ajar. There was no sound at all. Jean-Luc was scared. They couldn't be asleep. Maybe he'd killed them already? He felt sickness rise in his throat. He was very near to the door now, put out his hand and pushed it.

A piercing scream hit him and for a second he couldn't think straight and then a moment later, the two of them almost fell on top of him.

'Jean-Luc!' said Lauren panting. 'We thought it was him. We were trying to get away.' She looked at the door to the corridor. 'The guard will be coming in. He had a gun. The man outside.'

Simone looked frozen with shock.

'He's not outside any more.' Jean-Luc picked up the Glock and Lauren stared at the gun. 'Thank God, I didn't shoot you,' he said with a heavy sigh. 'No more talking while I

205

think what to do. The boss will be here in a minute and we haven't time to do anything you were planning.'

He looked at the vases on the floor.

'How do you know he's on his way?'

'Believe me, I know!'

'You're going to kill him, aren't you?' whispered Lauren.

'No, but I'm going to disable him. I'll be waiting for him. Problem is, I don't know what room he'll come into first. I daren't lock the door to my room because he knows the corridor door is open.' Jean-Luc looked round. 'The best thing for you two to do is hide behind the adjoining door. I'll stand near to it, so I can see which way he's coming in, then I'll let him have it. Whatever happens both of you, keep your nerve and don't give me away.'

'We won't.' He could see they were scared to death.

'Shouldn't we . . .? Oh!' They could hear footsteps in the corridor. Jean-Luc indicated them to move and they crouched as near to the wall as they could.

The door swung open and Jean-Luc had one second to recognise his prey—and fired. The boss roared and held his right shoulder. Jean-Luc fired again as the man cursed and yelled, trying to reach downwards, before he toppled backwards, head half in the corridor.

Jean-Luc ran over and held the gun pointing down at him.

206

The man's evil eyes were fixed on him. 'You'll pay for this,' he hissed and tried to wriggle away.

Jean-Luc caught hold of his legs and dragged him inside. He didn't want to shoot him again, but he kept wriggling, threatening to knock him off balance. Jean-Luc knew if the man did push him over, he would be able to find his gun first and then he'd be a goner and unable to protect the women.

Simone screamed at the third shot that Jean-Luc pumped into the man's leg. Lauren rushed forward and grabbed Jean-Luc's gun arm.

'That's enough, please!'

Jean-Luc staggered back, fighting off nausea. He could hardly believe what he'd done; shot a man three times in cold blood.

Lauren put her arms around him and he moved away from where the boss lay moaning.

'He's losing a lot of blood,' Lauren said. 'What shall we do?'

Jean-Luc came to his senses at last. 'I keep a first aid chest in my room. I'll go and get it. We'll bandage him up. He mustn't die!' Jean-Luc caught hold of Lauren. 'Paul told me to disable him, not kill him. He's up on the bridge re-enabling the GPS.'

'He's done it,' said a voice at the door.

Paul had come into the room silently, took off his hood and threw it on the bed.

'No need for that now. I've fixed it. The

team will be here soon. Now where's those bandages? I want him in court to pay for what he's done.'

Lauren and Jean-Luc watched as he dealt with the casualty, then went over to Maurice Belleville. After a few moments he came over and drew them aside, away from Simone.

'I don't think Belleville will make it, but who knows. It's not all over yet, so I need to prepare you for what might happen next. I've a feeling that I may have not quite managed to keep to time with the GPS and the bad guys might have launched their crafts. My team are on the way too, but we have to be prepared. I want the girls somewhere safe.'

'I'm not going anywhere,' said Lauren. 'I'll help.'

He smiled and for a moment, she saw a glimmer of her friend. 'Where's Gary?' she asked.

'In the hands of the law.'

'How?'

'Let's just say he walked into a trap. He's alright, but he has a hell of a lot of explaining to do and he won't get off lightly. He should choose his friends more carefully.' He grinned. 'Now, let's get on. We need to get up on the bridge. Jean-Luc, from now on you're in charge of the boat. Are you fit? You did a good job, by the way. You could be a soldier.'

'No, thanks,' Jean-Luc shook his head.

'Now,' said Paul quietly, 'Hostages always

have to be secured. I suggest sedating Simone and her dad. We can't put them with the others.'

'The others?' Lauren asked and Jean-Luc shook his head.

'Dealt with and down below,' Paul said. 'He comes with us,' he added, nodding to the boss man. 'I'm not taking my eyes off him and we might need him, but we need to tape him up.'

'I'll do that,' offered Lauren. Paul felt in one of his voluminous pockets and threw her a black roll.

'Don't cover his mouth, his breathing is bad.'

She knelt down, averting her eyes from the blood oozing from the three wounds, which Paul had fixed with tourniquets. The man was moaning, but his eyes were still filled with hate.

Paul glanced at her, 'You're a professional,' he added.

'This isn't the time for jokes,' she retorted.

Paul rummaged through the First Aid casket. 'Ah,' he said, 'Hypodermic kit . . . and blood. Yours, I presume?' he asked Jean-Luc. 'You rich lads know how to look after yourselves. He carries his own with him, Lauren. Just in case.'

'A precaution,' said Jean-Luc.

Lauren looked at them both with a puzzled expression.

'In case he's in some God-forsaken place

and needs a transfusion,' explained Paul. 'It's a good idea, just in case you ever need it,' Paul said. 'The only thing is we can't give it him. Let's hope he doesn't bleed to death. Now . . . ah, morphine. We could give Belleville a shot, but we have to be careful of the dose. It would make Simone drowsy, but too strong . . .' He was rummaging through the box again and produced a small bottle. 'Diazepam, great— that'll calm her down. See if you can get her to take a tablet, Lauren. It'll make her feel better.'

Lauren went to Simone with a glass of water and the tablet.

'What is it?' she asked.

'It'll make you feel better. We're going to the lifeboat now. You know I wouldn't give you anything to hurt you. I've looked after you, haven't I?' Simone nodded and gulped it down.

Lauren turned to Paul. 'I don't know where the lifeboat is.'

'We'll all take her,' said Jean-Luc. 'We have to carry Belleville and him anyway.'

'We have to be quick now. Bring the morphine. He might need it in the end. Come on,' Paul barked orders.

'I'll stay with him. You take Simone and her dad,' offered Lauren. She didn't fancy the idea but she knew she couldn't carry a man.

'You're sure? Back soon. Great work,' said Paul.

Jean-Luc quickly kissed her on the mouth. 'Back soon. Come on, Simone.'

She obeyed and they hoisted Belleville up and soon they were heading up the corridor, leaving Lauren alone with the gangster. She made herself look away from his face, though she knew he was trying to speak to her. She walked away and sat in the other room watching him through the door.

They were back soon.

'Was she alright?' said Lauren.

'Going off already,' replied Jean-Luc. 'They're covered in the tarpaulin. If the worse comes to the worst, we can get them down into the Med.'

'Not a good idea,' said Paul. 'Just in case the worst happens and I'm hit,' he added, 'I'll let you know the plan,' he said.

Until that moment, it had never occurred to Lauren that Paul might be killed. She watched as they hoisted up the bad guy.

Soon, they were on the bridge, which was bright with control panels and instrument lights. Jean-Luc was checking their location as Paul checked his watch.

'I don't know the team's location,' he said. 'I don't dare to make contact just in case. I can't set off thunder flashes, but they'll have our bearings and they'll be in a hurry. Now,' he handed over two Kevlar vests. 'One each. It might get rough.'

'Is it body armour?' asked Lauren.

'Sure is. You could take a full shot in the chest with this and you'll get knocked off your feet and stunned, but it won't penetrate. Here I'll show you,' Jean-Luc was putting his on while Paul was helping her with hers.

'I didn't know these were so heavy,' she said.

Paul nodded. 'They're not too bad, though with a full kit on and carrying a weapon, it's no fun.'

'Can I have a gun? Just in case.' She couldn't imagine shooting anyone, but if she had to, she would.

'Here,' he said, handing her one of the arms he'd collected.

'Where did you get these?'

'I unarmed the others of course.' Jean-Luc shot him a warning look. 'Careful now, I'll show you how. It's a bit different from trap-shooting.' He smiled at Jean-Luc.

'That sounds horrible,' said Lauren.

'Much safer though,' joked Paul, but the smile didn't quite reach his eyes. 'Now, put these on.' He produced two helmets which he handed over. 'Great, you look the part. Keep her on this course,' he said to Jean-Luc.

'Due east? Where?'

'I'll leave that your imagination. The inhabitants aren't friendly, but we can't deviate. The goons will know something's wrong,' said Paul. 'I've things to do.' They nodded. 'And remember, keep an eye on him.' He indicated the boss.

212

When he'd gone, Lauren got as close to Jean-Luc as she could. All she wanted to do was bury herself in his arms and forget everything. She knew he felt the same, because she could see the love in his eyes in spite of their predicament.

'Lauren,' he said. 'We're going to get through this—and when we do, we're going make a go of it.'

'I want to more than anything,' she replied.

'I know the captain doesn't usually kiss the First Officer, but he's going to.'

A moment later, the sweetness of their kiss dissolved as they broke apart when Paul ran in.

'Helicopters on the way—let's hope they're ours!'

They stared at him. 'You mean they have them too?'

'Maybe one. We'll soon find out. They'll be aiming for the bridge. Get down. We can't do anything now until we find out what's what. Take cover. I'll take him.'

They dived to the floor. The noise overhead shook the yacht and a strong light flooded the ship. Then the noise really started. They were suddenly under heavy gunfire.

'They're at it. Theirs must be here too. The 'copter's too loud for me to make out anything.'

Lauren closed her eyes and prayed. It went on and on. Jean-Luc was holding her very tight and she couldn't have coped without him. She just wanted to run.

'They're boarding,' said Paul as they heard loud knocking noises coming from the side of the yacht. 'Guns ready?'

Lauren could hardly hold hers steady, but Jean-Luc's fingers over hers steadied her hand and gave her strength.

'Don't shoot, until I give the order,' whispered Paul. 'We've still something to bargain with.' He nodded to the gang boss.

Moments later, Lauren watched the black boots striding across the floor. Next thing, she found herself staring into a rifle barrel. Then she heard the voice from outside . . .

'They're in here.'

She went weak with relief when she saw Paul gesticulating. 'Identification?' the voice demanded.

'HKRDEJD, 7524,' said Paul, edging his way forward, dragging the boss with him. 'I've got the boss here.'

'89543 DION,' was the response. 'Come on out of there, mate. It's all right, folks. I think we won the war.'

Paul showed a thumbs up. 'Dion?'

'Yep, you silly sod, come on out.'

They crawled out from under the console. The room was full of men in combat gear and the air smelt of maleness.

'We whopped them,' Dion said to Paul, then turned to look at Lauren. 'Come on out, we don't bite.'

Lauren was so relieved that she began to cry and was angry with herself. Jean-Luc held her close.

'Lauren James,' said Paul, identifying her to his colleague. 'Here,' he stretched out his hand. 'I'll take the gun.' She nodded and handed it over. 'And this is Jean-Luc Hilarie,' said Paul. 'He owns this rig and he's fairly handy with a weapon. We've got him to thank for this. And we have casualties. One here. Two in the lifeboat—gave the male morphine and the female Diazepam. They need hospital treatment. There are others.' He glanced at Lauren and the soldier nodded.

Some men ran forward and were picking up the boss, who was only half-conscious.

Dion nodded. 'Medic.' Two more soldiers came forward.

Dion looked at Jean-Luc and Lauren. 'Forgive me, but you two don't look so bright either. You need medical treatment.' He grinned. 'You're going to get a quick ride in a 'copter.'

'And my yacht?'

'We'll make sure she's brought in,' Dion said.

'They'll find whatever the gang were looking for. Now I have to go,' said Paul. 'Debrief. I'll see you both later.'

'Thank you,' said Lauren 'And there I only thought you were a good photographer.'

He nodded his head and laughed, then he

215

felt in his breast pocket. 'I nearly forgot to give you this.'

'My passport?'

'Yes, don't leave it lying around. Some detective might get hold of it.' He grinned.

Seconds later, Jean-Luc and Lauren were being ushered up onto the deck waiting to be winched up to the helicopter.

Lauren looked down at the Mediterranean, so shining and beautiful in the day time sun. A pall of smoke hung round *L'Hirondelle*, produced by the flaming wreckage of several speedboats. She could see a body floating in the water . . .

'Don't look, darling,' said Jean-Luc, 'You're safe now.'

CHAPTER TEN

Lauren didn't realise how upset she'd been by the whole traumatic incident until two days later when Jean-Luc fetched her out of the luxurious hospital, which in no way resembled her local NHS one at home.

He'd surprised her when she'd asked where they were going. 'A hotel I know,' he said. 'I didn't think you'd want to be reminded of The Hermitage, although Tante Catherine was very keen for you to come and stay with her.' His eyes twinkled.

Their destination turned out to be even grander, but on a smaller scale. When they walked in, Lauren said, 'Wow.'

'It's *fin de siecle*,' he said. 'All the best people used to come here—and still do.'

'I can see it's not part of a chain,' she said.

'Do you like it though? We're going up to the top.'

'How could I not like this?' She looked around. 'It's the penthouse suite, isn't it?'

She still couldn't get used to how wealthy he was.

'It's very exclusive. Invited guests only. The owner sees to it.'

'Who is the owner?' she asked, already knowing.

He shrugged. 'I am sorry, but I am, but I was going to sell it. If you like it, I'll keep it.' She stared at him—amazed. 'The penthouse is reserved for me,' he said.

She gasped. 'I don't what to say.'

'I do. You need to lie down. You look pale. You've been doing too much lately. Too much excitement.' When they reached the penthouse suite, Jean-Luc called out, 'Henri!'

A man entered.

'The usual, please,' Jean-Luc said.

'Yes, Mr Hilarie.' The man bowed and walked out.

'You have a butler?'

Jean-Luc made that little rueful gesture she was coming to love. ''Fraid so,' he said. 'But

I shall be giving him the night off. Come on. You need to rest.'

'I'm fine, Jean-Luc.' She looked round, lost for superlatives.

'The bedroom.' He was guiding her by the elbow, but she stopped. He looked at her with mischief in his eyes. 'What do you think?'

'What can I say?'

'Yes.'

'Yes.'

They walked through two rooms to get to it. It had the most amazing four poster. Somehow she hadn't expected that.

'It's almost as nice as the hospital,' she joked.

He shook his head and laughed.

'Have you forgotten something?' she said. 'We have a visitor in exactly . . .' she looked at her watch, '. . . ten minutes.'

They were expecting Paul.

'I remembered, but you need a quick nap.' She began to laugh at his expression, he was so charming. 'But afterwards, when we'll have more time . . .' His expression changed and made her heart flutter rapidly.

'Ah, Henri,' Jean-Luc said. The butler was standing very stiffly by the open door holding a tray. Jean-Luc went and took it from him. 'You can take the night off.'

'Oui, Monsieur Hilarie.' His face was expressionless as he retreated. Jean-Luc returned and poured some of the decanted

218

potion into a long-stemmed glass. 'Your favourite,' he said. Then he poured one for himself.

'What is it?'

'You remember the Coq d'Or? What was your favourite?'

'Bombe cassis?'

'Nearly right, but take my word for it, you'll love it. I'm not driving tonight.'

'Alright, I trust you.' She took a sip. 'I'm glad you're not.'

In fact, Lauren was so happy she would have drunk anything at that moment, thinking of what she knew was going to happen when Paul was gone.

*　　　*　　　*

Paul got the message. He looked like the Paul she'd known a few weeks ago.

'I don't want to hold you folks up,' he said, smiling. 'This is going to have to be brief. Now, Lauren, I'm afraid you might be called as a witness regarding Gary's affairs.' He held his hand up. 'Don't say anything. We know you knew nothing; it will be just a formality. The rest doesn't concern you legally. You were a victim, but again you'll have to go through some kind of inquiry regarding your ordeal. I can corroborate everything.

'Jean-Luc, I believe you have your solicitors on the case anyway. I'm sure you'll come off best, criminal damage and so on. Belleville is on his last legs, though it'll probably bc better if he doesn't come round—he's in it up to the neck.'

'What exactly did he do?' asked Lauren.

'He's been accepting dirty diamonds and selling them on. The gang who were his suppliers got wind of him shafting them and I'm afraid Gary was the prime mover in this. He was contemplating replacing them as Belleville's supplier.'

'I can't believe it!' said Lauren.

'I'm afraid it's true. I infiltrated Gary's business a long time ago and I've been playing his fool and getting him to rely on me. West Africa was the crunch, but you don't know the details and I'm not allowed to tell you.

'François was one of the gang and they decided that he'd be a plant on the yacht so they could get some of their remaining diamonds out. The only problem was, which he paid for dearly, he was greedy enough to double cross them, because he fell for Simone and wanted enough money to impress her.'

'What about her?' Jean-Luc asked.

Paul frowned. 'She'll be charged with the perversion of justice and might have to do time,' he replied.

They sat in silence for a few seconds. Then Jean-Luc nodded.

'And you'll have your yacht back in a couple of months, when they've been over it,' Paul added.

'Where were the diamonds?' asked Jean-Luc.

'In a big cheese in the fridge!' Paul laughed.

'A cheese?' said Lauren.

'A very large one, which was hollowed out In the middle to accommodate two kilos of diamonds.'

Lauren was amazed and couldn't think of anything to say.

That's about all for now, but I'll be in touch later, folks,' he said. 'I'm sorry I was so heavy-handed.'

Jean-Luc stood up. 'It's alright. Thank you,' he said, 'If it wasn't for you, we'd have been dead. Can I pay you . . .?'

'Not allowed,' said Paul, 'But a very nice gesture.'

They shook hands and he smiled over towards Lauren and added, 'You could invite me to the wedding, though!'

'Paul!' Lauren smiled in spite of herself and let Paul kiss her goodbye on both cheeks.

'You enjoy yourself—and don't do anything I wouldn't do.'

'That would take some beating,' she said.

'I assume you won't be leaving Monte Carlo for some time?'

Jean-Luc and Lauren nodded in unison.

'Well, make the most it before you go home. I'm off, but I'll catch you up some time. Maybe in court?'

Lauren put her arms round Paul and hugged him.

'You won't need me any more, Lauren,' he said, 'Not now you have someone else to take care of you and fight your battles. I've plenty more of those in the pipeline . . .'

He left the room and a few moments later they waved to him from the balcony and watched the car drive him away.

'Brave guy,' said Jean-Luc. Lauren nodded. 'But, as he said, we should make the most of it.'

His gaze drifted over to the enormous four poster bed and he grinned. 'Come here?'

Lauren ran into his arms happily.

His kiss was dizzying as his tongue explored her willing mouth and she felt her throbbing body melt into his. Her head was soaring and every fibre in her was straining against him. It was a glorious feeling.

He swept her up into his arms and carried her over to the four poster—but then he stopped, suddenly hesitant.

'Do you want to?' he said. 'You remember when we were in the garden and you said you wouldn't . . .?'

'Forget that, Jean-Luc. Believe me, I've never wanted anything more in my life!'

They lay down, facing each other and he began to undress her, slowly, deliciously, savouring every precious moment. She helped him as her desire increased in tandem with his, both knowing what they needed most, fully and completely.

At last they lay close, holding each other skin against skin and Lauren knew she never wanted to be anywhere else except with him. She had come home at last.